CONFESSIONS OF A JACKPINE SAVAGE

TWELVE SHORT STORIES

ROBERT MACGREGOR SHAW

BEAVER'S
POND
PRESS

Cover photo: Hunting shack, Koochiching County,
Minnesota circa 1972

ISBN 13: 978-1-59298-484-8

Library of Congress Catalog Number: 2012907233

Printed in the United States of America

First Printing: 2012

16   15   14   13   12   5   4   3   2   1

Book design and typesetting by James Monroe Design, LLC.

BEAVER'S
POND
PRESS

Beaver's Pond Press
7108 Ohms Lane
Edina, MN 55439–2129
(952) 829-8818
www.BeaversPondPress.com

To order, visit www.BeaversPondBooks.com
or call (800)-901-3480. Reseller discounts available.

Here's a toast to the big-hearted people of
International Falls, Minnesota
as I knew them in them in 1930's:
generous, independent, self-sufficient,
salt of the earth!

CONTENTS

Confessions of a Jackpine Savage

INTRODUCTION

The term *Jackpine Savage*, as I have heard it, describes people who live in northern Minnesota, Wisconsin, or perhaps a piece of Upper Michigan. They're forest people who stack their firewood in nice, neat piles behind their homes, survive sub-zero weather with heat from a barrel stove, and balance their diets by shooting, and eating, the occasional deer or grouse. They're reputed to be self-sufficient—solving their own problems, making their own entertainment—but suspicious of decisions handed down by outside bureaucrats.

That description now is way out of date, but it fairly describes the 1930s in my hometown, International Falls, Minnesota. I was there, and come by the appellation honestly: I am a Jackpine Savage.

The thirties, of course, was the time of the Great Depression. It was a bad time, but, strangely, I remember it as a *good* time, a time when people reached out and cared for each other. My father was a county agricultural agent who lost his job at the height of the Depression. That didn't prevent him and my mother at various times from taking under our roof a grandmother, a destitute aunt, an orphan, the husband of our "hired girl," and one or two other persons in desperate straits. Our neighbors were all doing the same: *taking care* of someone.

Memories of those days form the background and emotional setting for this collection. I wrote these stories over the years, sent some to my family and intimate friends, and filed them away. In 2011, I took them out, revised them, invented some more, and have published them with the help of the good people at Beaver's Pond Press. I present them now to you, and hope you enjoy them.

—Robert MacGregor Shaw, April 10, 2012

SEEDS TO REMEMBER

This particular day (it was in the mid-seventies, late summer) I came home from work, gave my wife a routine kiss, and mumbled a routine greeting which probably sounded like "Well, how'd it go today?"

"Been reading about Lake Superior," she said. "Lake Superior is the largest inland body of water."

I waited for the punch line, the humor, but nothing happened. She just stood there and looked at me. Wondering about this a bit, I sat down. She brought me a cup of coffee.

"Kids okay?" I asked.

"Willie skinned his right knee. Fell off his bike. Could have broken the patella but no—didn't break the skin so it's an abrasion, not a laceration. Painted it with ten percent Merthiolate and applied a four-inch compress bandage. He's had his tetanus shot."

I looked at her. Something had changed.

"You've got to take the car in for that lube job," she said, again without a smile. "It's 200, 300 miles overdue right now. Take it to Al's Body Shop. He's advertising a special price in the paper. We can save

3

six dollars and twenty-three cents."

First, Lake Superior, then ten percent Merthiolate, then $6.23. Strange.

"What's this about the car, Sweetie?" I said, "That's always been my department. And 'largest inland body of water'?"

"Oh, it's those spinach-seeds," she explained, reading my mind. Every year, she said, her grandmother would grind up spinach seeds and flowers, and store the gooey mess in the icebox.

I should mention that I'm a devoted vegetable gardener. Our back yard is not a grassy sward but a mass of black, loamy, fertilized earth that every summer displays nice, straight rows of radishes, kale, Swiss chard, bush beans, tomatoes, sweet corn, potatoes, and spinach. It was early September. Everything was trying hard to make seeds, working to perpetuate its species before the frost. We had been harvesting the tender little spinach leaves all summer, eating them raw with salad dressing. In August the spinach plants began to produce spikes with tiny flowers. At the base of each flower was a tiny black seed.

"So, you made a sort of broth from my spinach seeds, and you drank some of it?"

"Yes," she answered. "Saved it in the icebox. In a little white pitcher. Grandma always said spinach seeds were good for her memory. And if you remember, she had a terrific memory. Strange whirring sound emanating from the icebox," she said. "Better

4

check the warranty."

It's true that my wife's grandma did have a good memory about facts, and she also had the bad habit of talking about them all the *damned time*. Always an unending flow of little lectures with numbers, percentages, comparisons, data. No laughter, no smile, just that flow of information. Grandma drove everybody *nuts*.

But I was curious. After a rather dull supper, I decided to take a swig myself, just to see what it would do for my memory. The stuff was thick and tasted bitter. We went to bed early. I was not a believer.

I was swiftly converted the following morning. Whatever I looked at, it seemed, presented me with its life history. I looked at a big tree out of the window and clearly recalled the little maple sapling I planted there twenty years ago. I remembered not merely the event but the date, the botanical name of the tree, even the short-handled shovel I used to dig the hole. I looked across the street and saw not just a neighbor's house, but the whole *history* of that house. On the way to work I passed a stop sign that had recently been installed, replacing one that had been defaced. With no effort I was able to recall not only the defaced sign, but also the *previous* sign. You bet: There was power in those little bitty spinach seeds.

My improved recall really paid off that day at a board meeting. The chairman declared that the intent of a certain policy was such-and-such. I said no: The board, and he himself, originally had presented a much *different* intent. To make my point, I was able to recall dates, statements, even names of board members—several dead and gone—who were present at that critical meeting eight years in the past. My recitation of detail won the day. My stock rose in the company.

My wife, whose memory had never been very good, liked the effect of those spinach-seed cocktails. So did I. We decided to keep a supply in the icebox, every now and then taking a spoonful just to keep in shape.

As time rolled along, our world changed—some changes good, others not so good. We didn't make so many mistakes—you know, leaving keys in a lock, forgetting an appointment, misplacing a wallet. Everything worked like clockwork.

At the same time, our friends started to drift away. They didn't like "Lake Superior is the largest inland body of water" any more than I liked it on that first day. Our friends wanted warmth, imagination, *bonhomie*—not dull instruction. We were no longer invited out, and could not persuade guests to join us. Our conversations at home were deadly. If my wife said the glaciers were melting at two percent a year, I'd respond by pointing out that the oceans were warming at point eight, seven five.

It was a trade-off: the better the memory, the greater the isolation.

So one day we took that little white pitcher out of the icebox, emptied the contents down the drain, and started to live again.

Back to making mistakes. Back to missing appointments, forgetting to turn off my turn signals, forgetting birthdays and wedding dates. My wife, too, is back to her former self, making her own mistakes. When I come home from work I kiss her and *she kisses me back*. We joke and schmooze—even *dance*—just like the good old days. We're back to meeting and laughing with our friends, again, back with the human race.

I remain fascinated, though, with seeds. We know what poppy seeds will do: the good, the bad. We know that some seeds are poisonous. Some seeds—wheat, barley, oats—we eat. But if spinach seeds will increase one's memory, and poppy seeds will relieve pain, are there seeds somewhere that will improve our sense of humor? Enhance our imagination? Control our temper in heavy traffic? Make us more pious? See ourselves as others see us?

There's a world of seed-research out there, just waiting. Somebody should look into it.

BUBBA AND THE GERMAN HELMET

I have a friend, Ray Hamby, who is the publisher of a weekly newspaper, *The Herald*, in Struthers. Struthers is up in the northwest corner of Minnesota. I visited him not long ago in his office on press day, not the best to talk to the publisher of a weekly newspaper. There were many interruptions—printers asking questions about layout, the telephone ringing, visitors in clear sight wanting "a few minutes" to talk, the reporter—the *Herald* had only one—intervening from time to time.

"You're busy, Ray," I said, "be glad to come some other time!"

He shook his head and motioned for me to sit. "I've got a story," he said, "that could have happened only in a small town. Sit down, behave yourself, and listen." So I did.

I'm sure he intended that I should pass the story on to you.

"Well," he began, "the title of my story is 'Bubba and the German Helmet.'"

"Who's this Bubba?" I asked

9

"Just getting to that," Ray said. "When Bubba joined the Army just after Pearl Harbor he was a straight, smart young fellow just out of high school. Member of the National Honor Society, good athlete. He was assigned to the Big Red, the First Division, you know. He was at the Battle of the Bulge. Something awful must have happened to him there, because when he came back he couldn't talk right. His looked okay but when he tried to talk he'd just make loud, raucous sounds that didn't make any sense. Sometimes he'd shout, out of frustration, wave his hands in the air.

"After his parents died, folks tried to send him to a Veterans' Hospital, but he wouldn't go. His brain was all right. He proved that right away, he was no dummy. He just couldn't talk! No way were they going to send him to a hospital. He stayed in his parents' old house, just around the corner from here. Took care of himself pretty well.

"Well, Bubba got to be the town's handyman. Every day he'd come to the Border Café"—Ray pointed across the street—"and he'd sit at the same table and sort of 'take orders.' Have to move a piano? Talk to Bubba. Want somebody to spade up the vegetable garden? Talk to Bubba. Need a guy to shovel snow? Talk to Bubba."

"How'd he get that name 'Bubba'?" I asked

"Don't know, but that's what everybody called him: just Bubba. Not in a condescending way, though. After awhile we all in this town got to love the guy.

10

Well," Ray continued, "one day he was eating breakfast right over there at the Border, and a young guy roared into town on a great big motorcycle. Parked it just outside the restaurant, went in, sat down. Bubba was there, too. They both ate their breakfasts, and as it happened, both of them stood up at about the same time, paid the cashier for their meals, and went out the door.

"Well, right straight ahead was that motorcycle, and strapped to the motorcycle was a German army helmet. You know, some bikers used to think it was cool to wear a German helmet, maybe even paint a swastika on the side of it. This biker was just putting the helmet on, when Bubba started to scream and wave his arms. He stumbled across the sidewalk and ran headlong into the biker.

"The biker and his motorcycle went crashing down into the street. Bubba just stood there waving his fists, screaming, shouting, babbling. The biker got up and struck Bubba hard, right in the face. Bubba went down, blood running out of his nose. The biker then pulled up his machine, put on the helmet, got on his bike, and sped out of town.

"Bubba struggled to his feet, tears running down his cheeks, blood all over his face, and ran shouting after the biker, who by this time was roaring down the highway."

The *Herald*'s printing foreman came in, gave Ray a signal, and they both left the room. "Got to give the go-ahead," Ray said over his shoulder. "Press day, you know."

After about five minutes he returned and picked up the story.

"Now all this happened on a Saturday morning, busy time. That's the day when farm people come to town to shop, socialize, take a break. The sight of a bloody man running up the street caused cars to brake sharply and pull over to the curb. Some went right up on the sidewalk."

"'What happened? What set Bubba off?' people were asking. The answer was not long in coming, and spread through the crowd. 'It was that German helmet.'

"Well, we have a good chief of police in this town. Also a World War Two vet. He ran to his squad car, made a screeching three-block detour, pulled up ahead of Bubba, and got out. "'Come on, Pal,' the chief shouted. 'Come on! You know me, Bubba! Come on! Settle down!' Bubba paid no attention. Shouting incoherently, he passed the chief and continued down the street toward the edge of town.

"The chief ran after Bubba, overtook him, tackled him, and brought him crashing down to the pavement. A short ways away, a silent crowd collected to stare at Bubba sobbing on the ground, tears, blood, sputum covering his face and shirt. Both men lay there for about a minute, panting. Finally, our chief got to his feet, and pulled Bubba right up with him.

"'Good day for a parade, Bubba,' The chief said.

'Look, they're waiting for us! You and I, we're going to *make* a parade. We're going to *be* the parade!'

"So that's what they did," Ray said. "The chief left the squad car there to block traffic. The street was empty of cars, with lots of people standing on the sidewalks, sort of in shock. Both were well splattered with blood. Bubba stopped his babbling. The chief put on his hat. 'TEN-shun!' he shouted. Bubba straightened up. Then, staring straight ahead, the chief shouted, 'Forward-MARCH!'

"And back down our main street they came, the chief counting a slow, parade-like cadence: '*Hup. Hup. Hup.* Eyes straight ahead! *Hup. Hup. Hup.* Shoulders back! *Hup. Hup. Hup.*'

"The two of them marched," Ray said, "in perfect lock-step. About half of our town's population watched, in silence. Bubba held his head high, stared straight ahead. From the sidelines there came no shouts, no conversations, no clapping. Nobody even coughed as the two marched by.

"They marched down the main street," Ray said, "turned the corner, and ended at Bubba's house. Then some women from the Legion Auxiliary came in and washed Bubba, cleaned him up, took his bloody clothes away to be cleaned. And that was the day our whole town went home and cried.

"Our town, you know, is solidly Scandinavian. We don't show our emotions. We feel them just like everyone else does, but we don't like to *advertise* them.

So that day, all us good Scandinavians, we went inside, pulled down the shades, and got it all out. We cried for Bubba.

"Before they changed it to Veterans' Day, we used to have a big Remembrance Day parade here," Ray continued, "music, flags, high school band, majorettes, everybody cheering. And you know, that was wrong. What we needed, what every town needs, is a Bubba parade.

"Wouldn't it be a good idea," he continued, "for every town to find just one shot-up veteran—they're tucked away, out of sight, all over the place—and have an *honest* parade? John Philip Sousa's fine, makes you feel good. But just one time in the year, we should feel bad. Let everybody see what war does to people."

A siren went off. "Whoops!" Ray said, jumping up. "Got to check this out!"

"What happened to Bubba?" I asked.

"Well, nothing." Ray shrugged. "He was here half an hour ago. Goes to his apartment about this time of day. Keeps it neat as a pin. Saves his money."

Outside, a fire truck roared past. My friend, clutching his Rolleiflex camera, raced in pursuit down the street to get a picture, just in case.

THE PERFECT
PITCHMAN

The flu was running rampant in November 1990, and one of those vicious little viruses lodged in my right lung, multiplied, and laid me low. After an especially bad night of ferocious coughing, I drove myself to the clinic at Scandinavian Hospital. Following the receptionist's instructions, I tottered down the hall to the examination room.

A nurse came in, took my temperature and blood pressure, and left saying, "Dr. McPhee will be right with you."

When he arrived, Dr. McPhee was not quite what I expected. He was young, probably only two years out of medical school, five-foot-ten, and had red hair and a clipped beard.

"Dr. McPhee," he introduced himself, extending his hand to greet me. "Mr. Watkins, right?"

"Call me Fritz," I replied.

He nodded his head with a smile. "All right then, Fritz," he said. "Now let's see if we can find out what's giving your lungs so much trouble."

He glanced at a slip of paper that, I assumed, noted

15

my blood pressure and temperature.

"Bowels okay?"

Yes, I said, bowels were okay. No, I wasn't on any medications, no, I wasn't allergic to anything, no, I didn't smoke.

"Well, your signs look good, especially for a man your age." he said.

"And speaking as one of the oldest remaining bachelors, I hope I look good for my age, too!" I joked, my laughter tripping over a wheeze.

He swiveled around in his chair to study a screen. "Your history shows you've been pretty healthy, too. But let's take a look at your lungs. Take off your shirt and lie down."

He thumped my back a bit, striking the third finger of his left hand with two fingers of his right hand.

"That's G," I said. He stopped thumping.

"What did you say?"

"That's G," I repeated. "That tone you thumped is G."

"You mean when I percussed your back just now, you heard a tone?"

"Sure," I said. "I hear tones all the time."

"Are you a musician?"

I explained I was a retired high school music director.

"I used to be a musician myself," he said, brightening up. "Played Dixieland cornet. And you must be one of those people with absolute pitch! Tell me, what tones do you hear right now, in this room?"

"Well," I said, "that refrigerator over there is humming away in C. The telephone just rang in F. As for those nurses talking in the hall—the one doing most of the talking is in the B-natural range. The others are all over the place."

A nurse came in. "Your nine o'clock's waiting," she said.

"Got to go," he said. "But let's take an X-ray of your lungs. I think you've got some fluid in there."

"Yes," I said. "I know."

He paused in the doorway and walked back to the table. "What do you mean, 'you know'?"

"Because I heard two different tones in there. First one, a solid G. Second one, same tone, faint, but just a bit flat."

"Hm-m," Dr. McPhee said. He studied me and stroked the sides of his beard.

A young woman in a white coat came in from the next room, her blonde corkscrew ringlets gently bouncing with every step. Dr. McPhee rose to greet her.

"Mr. Watkins, I'd like you to meet Nurse Maxine Olsen," Dr. McPhee said. "Could you take Mr. Watkins to X-ray, Max?"

As she led me away, Dr. McPhee called after us, "Fritz? Will you hang around for a bit after the X-ray? I'd really like to talk to you. See what we can do with that bionic ear of yours."

"Don't let Andy bother you," Nurse Olsen

whispered. "He thinks he's funny."

Once I was zapped by the X-ray machine, I returned to the waiting room. I must have dozed off, because all of a sudden Max was standing in front of me holding the X-ray films. She helped me back to the examining room where Dr. McPhee was waiting.

"All right!" Dr. McPhee said. "Now let's take a look at your lungs." There was a little gap between his two upper teeth that made him look like a happy gopher when he smiled.

"Yes," he said, pointing to a cloudy corner of my lung, "you've got fluid in there, all right, but let me percuss you again and see what you can locate."

I lay down on the table, listening carefully while he thumped. "Okay, that's G . . . G . . . G," I called, head over the table, looking down at the floor. "Keep thumping toward the spine."

He thumped while I gave directions: "It's G . . . G . . . G—Whoops! Stop—right there! Different tone!" He made a mark on my back.

"All right," he said. "Now let's take a look at the film." Max placed my X-ray on the light panel.

"Matches perfectly," Dr. McPhee said softly, almost in a whisper. "Perfect match. The X-ray says the fluid's exactly where you say it is."

I sat up. "Dr. McPhee," I said, "I think I heard something else in there, but in a different spot. A bit northwest of the first one." I lay down on the table for another round of thumping. In less than a minute I had located another G-flat tone.

Dr. McPhee studied the X-ray on the panel, turned and studied the mark on my back, and continued going back and forth for several minutes, eyes wide open, mouth slightly ajar, fingers fiddling with his stethoscope.

"Fritz," he finally said. "I think you spotted something—fluid, most likely—that the X-ray didn't pick up. The X-ray only shows fluid in one area—you hear two."

He analyzed the X-ray for a minute longer before saying, "Max? Could you ring Dr. Schmidt in X-ray? Tell him I'd like to consult with him about a patient. Tomorrow, let's say 10:30 a.m., right here." Turning to me, he said, "I think we'd better keep you over-night. Do you think you could go home now, get a few things, and come right back?"

"Sure," I said.

As we walked down the hall, Maxine chuckled, looking at me with a twinkle in her eye. "You know, people in X-ray aren't going to be too keen about your discovery." Dr. Schmidt, she explained, was a "real bastard . . . a regular Boris Karloff."

The next morning we met again in the clinic. A tall, gaunt man in a white coat came into the room. "Dr. Schmidt, meet Fritz Watkins," said Dr. McPhee. "Dr. Schmidt's the head of our X-ray department."

This man—and he did look a bit like Boris Karloff—pulled the corners of his lips up and grunted something that sounded like "happy." I assumed my prone position on the table and looked down at the white tiles of the examination room, as several other white coats gathered around.

Dr. McPhee got right down to business. "Mr. Watkins here—retired high school music teacher—came in yesterday with an upper respiratory infection. No temperature, all other signs okay. Well, I percussed him and he started to identify the percussion sounds as musical notes on an eight-note scale. First, he heard only a musical G. When I percussed the area where the fluid was, though, he heard a slightly different, flatter G tone. I marked the area on his back. Take a look."

Everyone bent forward, hovering over the little mark on my back.

"Then," Dr. McPhee continued, "we took an X-ray of the same area. Take a minute to compare the two." All eyes shifted to the X-ray film on the light panel. "Take a look. See the fluid in the right lobe? Now, look at my mark on Mr. Watkins's back where he heard that off-G note. It looks like a perfect match!"

"Wait a minute. Going too fast," the cadaverous Dr. Schmidt growled in C-sharp.

"Okay, let me explain," Dr. McPhee said patiently, putting his hand on my shoulder. "Watkins here has what's known as absolute pitch. He hears sounds and relates them to musical tones."

"Tones? Tones? I still don't understand," Dr. Schmidt said, his voice rising. "Do you mean to tell me that somebody like what's-his-name—"

"Watkins is the name, Mr. Watkins," I said from my stretcher. Boris Karloff cleared his throat.

"—comes in here and he lays down—"

"Lies down," I said from the table. "Lies, not lays!"

I couldn't see Dr. Schmidt but I heard a sort-of gurgle as if he had something stuck in his throat. From among the white coats I heard someone snicker.

Dr. McPhee continued. "Mr. Watkins says he heard another G-flat in there. I marked it. See the mark? Over by the spine? It seems to mean that he detected fluid that didn't show up on the X-ray."

Ten, twenty more seconds of crashing silence.

"Fine, let's get another X-ray," Dr. Schmidt grumbled, turning abruptly and walking out of the room. The other white coats, too, moved out. Maxine helped me off the table and wheeled me after them down the hall. "Oh, that bastard, that bastard," she kept muttering through clenched teeth.

I got zapped again and Maxine pushed me back to the examination room. As we neared it, I heard loud voices. Dr. Schmidt had returned, and his voice was emphatic. "Dr. McPhee," he said, "to be quite frank, I am taken aback by your behavior. We can't assume he's got fluid in that second area. All we have to go off of is that this guy 'hears a different tone.' You mean to tell me that you would trust that over an X-ray?"

"All I'm saying, Dr. Schmidt," Dr. McPhee replied. "Is that we should *look into* this. It's clear to me that

Confessions of a Jackpine Savage

Watkins can locate fluid through sound. I want to know what *else* he can locate."

"You mean to tell me," Dr. Schmidt said, "that you're going to take somebody off the street—somebody with absolute pitch or whatever you call it—and use that as a diagnostic tool? Well, so long, Dr. McPhee. I'm not going to listen to this nonsense any farther!"

"Further," I called from the table. "Further, not farther."

The tall and sepulchral Dr. Schmidt stalked out of the room, throwing a pestilential glance over his shoulder.

Then there were only three of us—Dr. McPhee, Maxine, and me—in the room. Dr. McPhee looked at me and, flashing his happy gopher smile, laughed uproariously in high C. "And you corrected his grammar, not once, but twice!" he exclaimed, shaking his head. "Not once, but *twice*! Nobody around here does that—nobody! And not once, but *twice*!"

Regaining control, he wiped his eyes and gave me a serious look. "Fritz, I think Dr. Schmidt would like to stop our research."

"I picked up on that, Dr. McPhee," I said.

"Call me Andy," he said. "And I'll call you Fritz. And we'll both call her Max. Okay?"

He stood up and looked out of the window. "You know, this could be *really* important. If people with your gift could hear things before they show up on X-rays, that could have big implications, real big implications. You've got me all shook up, Fritz."

"Shaken," I said. "Shaken."

"All right, shaken, then," he said. "Max: I'd like to find out if Fritz can locate tumors. Could you set something up for tomorrow afternoon? Get a patient who's got tumors. Be sure to sign the papers. Let's see what else he can do."

Maxine reserved the hospital's boardroom for a demonstration. Ten staff members were invited, as well as the director of the university's medical school. In the written invitations, Dr. McPhee laid out the situation clearly: "I have a patient who has absolute pitch. He is extremely sensitive to sounds. He has demonstrated that he can locate pulmonary fluid by listening to very slight changes in tone from my auscultation. The purpose of our meeting is to determine what else he can locate."

Everyone who was invited showed up promptly on the scheduled day in the clinic's boardroom. Alex Dodge of the clinic's public relations staff and a writer for the *New England Journal of Medicine* also appeared.

I arrived about an hour early. Andy was already there. Max was there too, setting up a little table with coffee and nametags. There was an examination table in front, surrounded by two rows of chairs.

Guests started to arrive and Andy, in his open and friendly way, greeted them all. The room echoed with sociable laughter and talk. Maxine showed guests to their seats.

Andy stepped to the front, smiled his gopher smile, and waited for the talk to subside.

"Welcome," he said. "Welcome to my informal, unrecorded, unprecedented little test!"

He introduced several of his colleagues, including Dr. Schmidt.

"And now!" he said with a flourish, "May I present Mr. Fritz Watkins, a retired teacher of music, a man with absolute pitch!"

I faced the crowd and smiled apologetically, as if to say, "Okay, it's true. I've got perfect pitch. Got athlete's foot, too."

"Mr. Watkins came in with a cough three days ago," Andy continued. "Same upper-respiratory stuff we've been seeing a lot of lately. Had a slight temperature, all other signs okay. I sent him down for an X-ray—and here it is." He pressed a button and my X-ray appeared on a large, lighted screen. It clearly showed a patch of fluid on the upper lobe of my right lung.

"I think you can see why he was coughing," he said. There was a shuffling of chairs as people moved to get a closer look.

"Well, I percussed Mr. Watkins," Andy went on. "And right away he said he heard a tone. He said he heard G. You know—G, the fifth note on an eight-note scale. But then he said he heard a different tone, slightly off G, flatter than the rest. I marked the location of that off tone on his back."

"Mr. Watkins, please stand up and show them

your back." I did so.

"Look for yourself—my mark and the X-ray seem to match perfectly."

There was more shuffling of feet as the white-coated audience members moved around the panel.

"But," Andy said, lightly touching my back. "There is something even more significant. Mr. Watkins heard the same tone much more faintly in *another* spot. I marked that area, too . . . right there, over by the spine."

More scraping of chairs and shuffling of feet.

"And here's the point—that second area didn't show up on any X-ray!" All of the guests now had risen from their chairs and surrounded the table.

"Now this raises several questions," Andy continued. "If a person with absolute pitch can hear fluid before we can find it with X-rays, what other abnormalities can he find? And how soon?" Nobody spoke. It was a moment of rhetorical silence.

Nurse Olson, he explained, would bring in several patients, each with a different problem. He would percuss, I would listen, he would mark, and we would compare my marks with patients' X-rays. I would not be able to see the X-rays.

Max left and returned wheeling a middle-aged man on a stretcher. Andy announced: "Mr. Sorensen from International Falls!"

Mr. Sorensen lay facedown on the table. Maxine hoisted his X-ray.

"You can see the problem," Andy said, pointing to the film. "Now, I'll percuss."

He thumped the man's lower back. "It's F . . . F . . ." Suddenly the tone fell to F sharp. "Stop, mark!" I said. Andy made a small X with a felt-tipped pen on Mr. Sorenson's back.

I heard shoes shuffling as our white-coated guests gathered to compare Mr. Sorenson's X-rays with Andy's mark. It had taken about ten thumps for me to locate a stone in Mr. Sorenson's right kidney.

"Next!" Andy called. Max wheeled in Adolph Peterson from Bismarck, North Dakota. Mr. Peterson got up on the table.

"Now again," Andy said. "I'll percuss, Mr. Watkins will listen, and I'll mark." He proceeded to thump Mr. Peterson's lower back. "D . . . D . . . D . . ." I said, but then I heard a dull thud in C. "Mark, please," I said. Out went Mr. Peterson.

"Tumor in the bladder," Andy said. "Mr. Watkins located it in less than a minute."

I heard a faint,"Well I'll be damned."

Next came Mrs. Cunningham from Duluth. Maxine affixed the X-rays, Andy thumped her neck. I heard one sound, then a second. "Mark!" I called. Andy marked. Out went Mrs. Cunningham.

"Ninety percent blockage in the carotid artery," Andy said. "Mr. Watkins located it in thirty seconds."

In the following half hour I was able to locate calcified tubercles in an old woman's lungs, a malignant tumor in a man's liver, two bits of shrapnel in the shoulder of a WWII army veteran, and an ulcer in the stomach of a CEO.

"What does all this mean?" Andy probed. "Do we have something here that will simplify, speed up, and improve our work? Enable us to accurately diagnose more people at a faster rate? Let's face it, most people in this world—many people in our own country—don't have easy access to X-ray machines. If they do have the access, they can't afford the diagnosis. When something goes wrong, they sit and wait and pray, and only *when it really starts to hurt* do they go to see the doctor. And then it's too late. It is my belief that we can use individuals like Mr. Watkins with perfect pitch to perform preventative medicine, diagnosing patients before X-ray services would typically be called upon, and potentially with more accurate results."

There was another pregnant pause while Andy let his words permeate the room. "Any questions?" Andy finally asked. Nobody had questions.

After a moment, Professor Elend of the medical school took the lead, rising to his feet. "I must admit," he said, "I am impressed. But first, Dr. McPhee, we'll need a lot more evidence. A lot more data."

"I hope that we'll get it," Andy said, flashing his gopher smile.

There were approving murmurs throughout the crowd.

"Well, thank you all for coming!" Andy said in his

merry way as the guests filed out of the room.

What a strange presentation, I thought. Andy seemed to play this for entertainment, for fun! It didn't seem like medicine, didn't feel like science. Soon the room was empty except for me, Andy, Max, and the reporter from the *New England Journal of Medicine*.

"It's going to be a hard sell," the journalist said. "I really believe you're on to something, could be big. But we're not going to publish anything until you do some more testing. You haven't proven, you know, that Mr. Watkins can locate abnormalities before X-rays can. All you know is that he hears a different tone."

Andy thanked him for coming, and the journalist took his leave.

Andy turned to me. "Well, what do you think, Fritz? At least you didn't correct anybody's grammar today."

As I tied my shoes, I had a down-to-earth thought: Should I ask for money—enough, perhaps, to pay for my gas and oil? I asked. Andy smiled warmly at me, and said he knew of a foundation that might give us a grant. "It might take some time, though, so until we get some help I'll pay you out of my own pocket. How about $35 an hour to start? Let's say mornings, from 7:00 to 8:00 a.m.?"

"That would be fine," I said. Oh yes! Thirty-five dollars an hour would be very, very fine.

Something brand-new had come into my life. No longer did I feel like an old bachelor isolated in his shabby one-bedroom apartment. I had been blessed with a brand-new status. I was Exhibit A in medical research, star of the show!

The next morning we were surprised—*shocked* is a better word—to see a story in the Minneapolis *Star Tribune* with a two-column headline: "Locate Cancer With Tones?" The question mark, of course, conveyed a typographic skepticism. Here, folks, here comes another cure for cancer . . . but with tones?

Written by H. P. Bjornson, the *Star Tribune*'s science reporter, the article mentioned "Dr. Andrew McPhee" and "a retired high school teacher named Frederick E. Watkins." The story was a straight, factual summary of our demonstration the previous day in Scandinavian Hospital's clinic. It appeared to be an account by an eyewitness.

I was credited as a person with absolute pitch ("persons with extreme sensitivity to sounds") and the uncanny ability to locate the presence of out-of-place fluids, kidney stones, tumors, stomach ulcers, and signs of early tuberculosis in the human body.

In spite of the skeptical headline, which was not written by Bjornson but by some cynical copy editor, the article suggested that tonal auscultation—a term coined by Bjornson—might serve as an important diagnostic tool for the early detection of tumors.

However, a nagging question remained: who leaked the story to the Tribune? I was certain that it wasn't the man from the *New England Journal of Medicine,* who was known as a very conservative and careful professional journalist. Was it one of the clinic's staff?

I arrived at the clinic just as the storm broke.

The clinic's telephones were jammed. The Associated Press had picked up Bjornson's story and put it on its national wire, so the whole world knew about "a possible breakthrough in the early detection of cancer." The Associated Press was on the phone again, and so were the *New York Times*, the Indian Embassy in Washington, D.C., the medical-insurance professionals, and many cancer victims. Everyone wanted to know more. The story, as they say, had legs—great, big legs. Early detection was a hot issue.

I successfully circumvented a gathering of white coats and raised voices just outside the business office. Andy was surrounded by Dr. Schmidt and a few cohorts from X-ray.

Andy came in, locked the door, and sat down. "Wow!" he said. "They think I did it. They think I leaked the story! You've read it, haven't you? It had to be somebody who was there . . . Fritz, come on—did you do it?"

"No," I said. "Absolutely not. I swear I did not call the press."

"Well, I didn't either," he said. "It must have been one of the staff."

The storm gained momentum throughout the morning. Schmidt and Dodge posted statements on the bulletin board in the coffee shop denying their complicity. Andy called H. P. Bjornson requesting the source. Bjornson, of course, refused to disclose it. By the end of the day, everyone in the clinic was fairly sure that Andy—the one who, after all, had invited the *New England Journal of Medicine* to see his demonstration—had done the deed.

At around nine o'clock the following day a call came in for Andy from the Medical Board. "I'd better take that one," he said.

It didn't seem convenient to stick around. I departed, and as I came out the rear door I saw a big TV truck pulling into the parking lot. Broadcasters had picked up on the scent.

Later that morning, Andy called to tell me that the medical licensing board was interested in scheduling a visit to learn about tonal auscultation. On three successive days Andy and I met with them to demonstrate that I could detect certain abnormalities by listening to sounds. Andy was careful to emphasize that our work was only a secondary diagnostic tool, merely an adjunct. At the same time, he felt it was not propitious to mention our major finding: our belief that tonal auscultation could find certain problems even *before* X-rays could.

The board people, represented by a smart, young lawyer, asked about the leak to the *Star Tribune*. No, Andy insisted, those words were Bjornson's, not his. The lawyer made notes and the board took their leave.

The next day I came to the clinic at 7:00 a.m. to

continue our research. Andy and Max were already there. I immediately sensed that something was wrong. Max was sitting in a chair, Andy was standing behind it, and he had his hand on her back. I noticed black blotches on her starched uniform. She had been crying. After a very long moment she took a shaky breath. "I did it, Fritz. H. P. Bjornson down at the *Star Tribune* is my uncle. Uncle Harry."

Andy, trying to comfort her, kept saying, "It's all right, Max. We'll be all right. I won't say anything, Max. Don't worry."

"No," she said, "No, Andy. Why should you take the blame?"

"We'll let them guess," he said. "We'll just let them guess."

Something heroic took shape before my eyes that morning in the examination room. Andy was determined to protect Maxine, even at the expense of his own career.

For several days we continued our early morning research. Maxine wheeled patients in and out, Andy thumped, I called the tones, Maxine kept records, and each day we accumulated more data. We worked from seven until eight when Andy and Maxine proceeded with their regular work at the clinic, and I went home.

It didn't take very long for Andy to discover that he wasn't welcome at the clinic any more. As a doctor, close cooperation with the people in X-ray was essential, especially in emergencies. Now, reports that used to come back in a few minutes took hours. Sometimes Andy himself had to walk down the hall to get results.

"They're trying to freeze me out," he said when we met early one morning. "Schmidt's freezing me out. He's passed the word."

"The bastard," Maxine said softly. "Why should you suffer, Andy? I'm the one who caused all this."

"No, Max," Andy responded. "No. It's more, it's deeper than that piece in the paper. What we're doing doesn't look professional. We're renegades. We use untrained people to do our work. They can't stand to see something quicker, better, cheaper come along. As Schmidt said, we take some guy . . ."

"Right off the street," I interrupted.

"Sure. No training, no accreditation, no license, no nothing, and that's all that matters to Schmidt."

Two weeks after the newspaper story, Andy decided to leave the clinic. Maxine said she'd resign and go along. I'd go, too.

So the next day, we packed up our things and walked out the door. We were on our own. Nobody had a good-bye party for us, but Bjornson was on the story, and announced our departure with the headline: "Controversial M.D. Leaves Clinic at Scandinavian."

For the next two weeks we met every morning in Andy's basement, making plans to open our own office. We decided to organize our firm as a cooperative. We'd sell non-transferable shares—to patients only—with a limit of five shares per patient. Max did all the paperwork.

Appointments for exams would not be necessary. We decided to charge a flat fee of $25 for each examination. Andy would percuss, recording comments as he worked. I, of course, would listen for off-tones while Andy made marks. On the way out, Max would give patients a typed transcript of Andy's analysis to take to their doctors. We were to be equal, three-way partners, and named our clinic The Tonal Auscultation Clinic.

We opened up for business on the tenth floor of an office building opposite city hall in downtown Minneapolis. There was plenty of parking in the basement. After minimal renovations we moved in, an event duly noticed in the *Star Tribune* by H.P. Bjornson: "Tonal Thumpers Set Up Independent Shop; Open for Business."

Patients immediately started to arrive. We had only one thump-team, Andy and I, and immediately found that we needed more. At our current rate, we could only auscultate twenty to thirty patients a day. Our waiting room was packed, standing room only, and we were turning patients away. There were traffic jams outside the building. Management was unhappy.

News reporters and photographers were always welcome, and they said some very nice things about our work. Our $25 thumping fee got a lot of attention. Bjornson helpfully compared it to the standard $150 per-X-ray charge paid by the American taxpayer to Medicare.

More important than the money, though, was the fact that every day we were able to uncover previously undetected problems, some of them life threatening, and send the patients along for further treatment.

In the spirit of science, we devoted our afternoons to demonstrations for medical teams that came to learn about what we were doing. We charged a flat $500 per demonstration. China, Nigeria, Egypt, and South Korea all sent groups of physicians to investigate. Hillary Clinton, our First Lady who was working on her own proposals to reform the American healthcare system, called from Washington, D.C., and sent some staff members over to observe us at work. Four physicians from New Delhi, India, flew in, observed a demonstration, and invited us to come to India to demonstrate our technique, all expenses paid.

To one and all, Andy always gave a clear, consistent message: "Early detection, that's all we do! We find, we refer."

All along, though, I sensed ambivalence about our work. It took me a while to realize the cause of this. While medical professionals accepted the substance of our work, many could not get beyond the form. To many, I'm sure, our work seemed like show biz.

The young Dr. McPhee with his cheerful, bearded face was rapidly becoming a Robin Hood character, the heroic, independent soul who breaks away from the establishment. Bjornson and other writers didn't help.

Correctly sensing the latent conflict with the medical establishment, they fanned the flames with phrases like "breakthrough in the fight against cancer" and "grass-roots challenge to the medical establishment."

Andy, Max, and I worked smoothly as a team; Maxine met patients at the door, directed them to the changing booths, schmoozed with them as they waited, and recorded the data. Andy thumped away and recorded observations on his throat mike.

Patients started coming from Wisconsin and Iowa, even as far as Montana, for our $25 thump sessions. Business was booming. We advertised widely for people with absolute pitch, and they came! We recruited more doctors and nurses to thump. Soon we had three teams working full-time. H. P. Bjornson of the *Star Tribune* published a consistently sympathetic report of our work.

After six weeks of frantic activity in the downtown location, we found we had to move. We were swamped, and at our current size, we couldn't handle all of the patients. Maxine looked around, and found an empty building recently vacated by a large food store in one of the suburbs. With a fresh coat of paint, a few partitions, and the installation of three telephone lines it was quickly transformed into the new home for our Tonal Auscultation Clinic.

We were also making lots of money. Visiting dignitaries didn't mind paying the $500 fee for a demonstration, and there seemed to be no end to patients who were happy to pay $25 for a life-saving glimpse into their future ailments.

We were happy, we were making money, but above all: every day we were discovering early signs of tumors and other serious ailments and directing patients to receive medical care.

If Andy hadn't been such a ham, we'd probably still be in business.

Since spending so much time listening to the human body, I had learned the unique tones of internal organs and made a scale of them. Lung tissue always thumped in G. Heart, anybody's heart, always gave C. Bladder was in D, liver in F, and kidneys E. Pancreas always resonated in A, spleen in B. Based on this information, Andy invented a compact device that fit on his thumping finger. Assisted by a filter and a small speaker, he was able to play a musical scale. He called this new instrument the "Somaphone." From time to time, he'd hook up his little amplifier and we'd have a private jam session, right on my back. We'd play *Saints*, *Sweet Georgia Brown*, and *St. James Infirmary*, good, old, traditional Dixieland numbers.

Well, Andy just couldn't help himself—he had to show his little device to an audience. One Saturday night, he played the Somaphone at his medical fraternity over at the University. I was the thumpee. The crowd—all medical students—loved it. Somebody took a flash photo and sent it to the *Star Tribune*. H. P. Bjornson, our pal, was on vacation that week, and his place unfortunately was taken by a prissy, pretentious hack by the name of Von Buffing. His review of the episode, resplendent with the photo of Andy on the vibes, caused a mighty uproar.

That photo of Andy belting out *Saints* on my back trivialized and destroyed every good thing we had tried to do with tonal auscultation. There was a flood of outraged letters to the editor. Editorial writers and columnists joined the fray.

People from the Medical Licensing Board, who for a long time had been bothered by tonal auscultation, soon were knocking at our door again.

At our morning meeting three days later, our receptionist handed Andy a letter from the medical board. We knew what was in it. Nobody spoke. Andy read the letter, put it down on the table, slowly closed his eyes and stroked his beard as he had done when he had first recognized the potential of my perfect pitch.

Maxine, sitting directly across the table, rose, walked behind Andy's chair, and read the letter. Then she put one hand on Andy's shoulder, bent down and placed her head against his, and left it there for one long minute. Andy reached up and placed one of his hands over hers. This lasted just a few seconds, but for the first time, I saw that Maxine loved Andy and that Andy loved Maxine.

"This time they're really shutting us down," Andy said. "Unprofessional conduct. I can't practice medicine without a license."

"Don't worry, Andy," Maxine said. "Don't worry, Andy. We'll make it. We'll stay together."

The next morning a sheriff's deputy drove up and taped an official-looking document and yellow tape across the entrance to our front door. I spent most of the day standing out front, turning patients away. Yes, we were out of business. Yes, Dr. McPhee had lost his license to practice medicine. No, no more $25 examinations. A TV truck rolled up, interviewed us, and left. On the ten o'clock news, they quoted our friend, H.P. Bjornson of the *Star Tribune*. "A tragedy for medicine for the masses," he wrote. "Bye-bye to preventive medicine. Now, back to the same old rule: don't go to the doctor unless something hurts."

There was a flurry of letters to the editor in our defense. A few of our patients showed up with signs at the Medical Practices Board in St. Paul. Most of our supporters, though, were old, and it was cold outside, so when the media paid no attention our activists soon went home.

Andy, though, knew what to do. "Call those people from India," he said. "The ones who invited us to come over for a demonstration."

I called the ambassador from the Republic of India at the embassy in Washington D.C.

"We've been following your work on tonal auscultation," he said. "Come to New Delhi. We'll pay all expenses. We want to observe what you do."

Arrangements were swiftly made to fly to New

Delhi, and on a brilliant September day Andy, Maxine, and I flew to Chicago, got on another plane, and left the United States for India.

Once again, to a rapt audience of about 100 physicians, I demonstrated that I could locate abnormalities—in particular, tumors. The Indian authorities made a bold offer: "Stay with us. Teach us how to do it. We need you! We have millions of people with no access to X-ray machines."

And that, of course, is what we did. We went to India.

In the two years since we came we have located thousands, hundreds of thousands of serious problems and sent them on for treatment. We have about 200 auscultation teams, each one composed of a person with perfect pitch and an Indian licensed nurse doing the thumping. If a patient can't afford the two rupees—six, seven cents—for an exam, he or she can pay by working half a day in the community vegetable garden.

We miss Minnesota, that happy land with its eleven thousand sky-blue lakes. We go back every summer, tell people what we're doing, and every time our colleagues remind us that we're practicing socialism. Whatever they call it, it has given me deep satisfaction, a life of purpose.

THE COURTEOUS RECEPTIONIST

I was seventy-six years old, not too well, and I decided it was time to make several changes in my will. On a very windy day in March I boarded a city bus, alighted in downtown Minneapolis, found my lawyer's building, and went to the top floor.

As I entered the room, I was pleased to see a pretty young woman sitting behind a large and shiny desk.

"Good morning!" I said.

"Moody, Purdy and Shirk," she said to somebody on the horizon. "If you have a legal question, say 'legal.' If you wish to discuss your account, say 'account.' If you know the name of the person with whom you wish to speak, say his or her first or last name."

"Good morning!" I said again.

"If you have a legal question—" she said, looking straight at me.

"No, no," I interrupted. "Just want to talk to Mr. Moody, that's all."

She didn't stop, but kept talking until the very end of her spiel, "—say his or her first or last name." Then she pressed a button. "Please take a seat." I sat.

The Moody, Purdy and Shirk waiting room was full and overflowing. I listened, we all listened, to at least a dozen "if you have a legal question" routines. A young man standing in the rear broke the magic of the moment. "Jesus!" he shouted. "Can't somebody stop her? Shut her off?"

Now the receptionist's eyeballs were receding upward into her head, exposing a whitish area without pupils. Her voice grew louder, deeper, raspier. "IF YOU HAVE A LEGAL QUESTION," she screamed, "LEGAL QUESTION LEGALQUESTION *LEGAL LEGAL LEGAL!*"

Two workmen rushed in. To my absolute horror, one of them lifted a small flap on the back of the receptionist's head and withdrew what appeared to be a tiny black panel. The other workman twisted a valve on her neck. There was a loud hissing sound. The workmen heaved the beautiful young receptionist into a cart as she began to shrink and collapse. I got a glimpse of a metal skeleton among the bundle of limp, skin-colored integument as they rushed out.

Mr. Moody himself came out. We went into his office. "Boy, that's some receptionist you've got," I said.

"Oh, that's Nora. She saves the firm a lot of time. Time, you know, is the lawyer's stock in trade. Abraham Lincoln himself said that. We did a study and found that most talk with the public around here uses the same old linguistic building blocks, clichés like, 'if it isn't too much trouble,' 'I beg your pardon.' Great waste of time. Even 'Good morning' and 'Merry

Christmas.' Nora heads them off at the pass. Saves us a lot of useless schmoozing."

"She seemed to get stuck today," I said.

"She'll do that every now and then. Gets her wires crossed."

Unbelievably, Moody's eyes were gradually ascending up into his head—another white-eyed ghoul. What was it about this place?

"It's just a matter of our time!" he shouted. "A lawyer's time is his stock in trade! Abraham Lincoln! STOCK IN TRADE," he screamed. "STOCK! IN! TRADE!"

I beat, as they say, a hasty retreat while the same two workmen rushed in. "Wow! Two in one day," I heard one of them mutter.

Scoping
Mrs. Nelson

International Falls, that city on the northern border of Minnesota, is all by itself, up there. The only comparable community—except for Fort Frances, Ontario, across the Rainy River—is Virginia, about 100 miles south, in what we call the Iron Range.

Everybody knows about Bronko Nagurski, our town's favorite son. When he played for the Chicago Bears, they say, Bronko was the only fullback in history who could run his own interference. After football and wrestling, Bronko ran a Pure Oil gas station near the end of Third Street. One day, so the story goes, two smart-ass college kids drove in to get some gas, and needled Bronko a bit as he filled up their tank. He didn't say a word, but he screwed the cap so tight on their tank they never could get it off again. Bronko was awfully big, but he also was gentle. People in the Falls still love to talk about him, remember him. That man, I tell you, had arms as big as most people's legs.

Of course, there's the cold. For about six months citizens in the Falls take cold weather pretty much for granted, but when a stiff north wind brings minus thirty-or forty-degree temperatures to town, people draw close, tend to watch out for each other. Old Mr. Johnson, a bachelor farmer, gets a call from a neighbor just to see he's all right. People in nursing homes get long-distance telephone calls from their grandchildren, just checking. These same old folks telephone their children to make sure the grandkids have warm mitts. Firemen pray, "Please, God, no fires tonight!" Winter makes people in my town reach out, put their arms around each other, care for each other.

The Falls didn't smell very good in the thirties, while I was growing up. Sulphides from the paper mill created a strong rotten-egg odor. Every day, with a helpful north wind, the mill spread majestic clouds of that stuff over town. You could cough and complain about this, but if you did somebody would straighten you out right away. "That's the smell of prosperity," he'd say. "When you can't smell it, we're all in trouble!" Thanks to that smell, the M&O—Minnesota and Ontario Paper Company—carried our town right through the Depression, every weekday shipping huge rolls of newsprint and flat insulating board south to the Twin Cities. Our beautiful Rainy River in the thirties was shamefully polluted with untreated effluent from our town's sewer system. Fish couldn't live in the river, downstream from the dam. Nobody swam in it.

My town was a pretty rough place in the thirties, while I was growing up. When the Eighteenth

Amendment was repealed, two blocks of bars on Third Street, our main drag, joyously opened their doors for business. Every weekend, hundreds of lumberjacks from a vast area came to town for cultural pursuits, which included getting drunk and visiting prostitutes sequestered over on Second Street, little red lights glowing from their windows.

In 1930 I was eight years old, and in that year sex became a favorite topic among my fourth-grade classmates at school.

We knew that something secret was going on among adults, we weren't sure just what it was. Two schools of thought emerged. Oscar Bergstrand, a big, strong farm boy, was the spokesman for the "people do it" faction. "Sure they do it!" he'd declare. "Everybody does it! Everything in the world does it!" I was the spokesman for the other side, insisting that my parents did not "do it." Oscar made my life miserable. "Your parents *especially* do it!" he'd shout at me during recess. "They do it, do it, do it!"

From hearing certain creaks, bumps, and laughter from my folks' bedroom I had already figured out that something private and pleasant was occurring behind locked doors. I couldn't help but notice how dogs hunched each other in a congenial and cooperative way. What were they doing? What was going on?

On our first Cub Scout hike that spring, we walked along a barbed-wire fence right past a cow and bull joined together in what seemed to be the same sort of cooperative action. Earlier in the hike, Mr. Foster, our Cub master, had pointed out all sorts of interesting things, but as we walked twenty feet past these huge, copulating beasts he made no comment, eyes fixed to the trail. This caused some merriment among the troops. I could see that Mr. Foster was embarrassed, but embarrassed about what?

My parents owned one of the tallest buildings in town; a ramshackle, four-story building in the business district of the Falls. Nothing much happened over the first floor, where I lived, and ran a small restaurant. I should say my mother ran the restaurant. At the battle of Château-Thierry in 1919, my father took one whiff of mustard gas, and for the rest of his life he took very small steps and lived in a wheelchair.

My mother, therefore, did all the work. Which was fine with her. She liked people, and they liked her. They liked to drop in to our café to get out of the cold, eat a piece of pie *à la mode*, schmooze a bit, and pick up the latest gossip. Old colleagues and former students—mother had previously been a teacher—dropped in. Our restaurant was one of the main social centers on Third Street, our "main drag."

On a bright May morning in 1933, just four days before our annual Paul Bunyan Festival, a tall woman with long red hair walked into our restaurant, looked around, unbuttoned a big raccoon coat, hung it up on the rack, picked up a copy of the *Daily Journal*, sat down, and began to read.

I was in the back room, peeling potatoes, and examined her through a crack in the door. That day our paper, the *Daily Journal*, had a picture of Hitler on the front page. There were people back then, you know, who thought Hitler was okay. Wasn't he building highways, putting people to work, talking peace? There was a second photo: our governor's, Floyd B. Olson, with good wishes for International Falls's Paul Bunyan Day.

The red-haired lady laughed. Wow! That voice! It was Jean Arthur's voice, musical and low, tuned I would say, in about A flat. You remember Jean Arthur, don't you? She starred with Gary Cooper in *The Plainsman*.

Mother had just come in from the kitchen. "What's this problem with Bemidji?" Jean Arthur said.

Mother moved to the table and sat down, the way she liked to do with customers. "Oh, Bemidji's just a hick town 100 miles down south. Watch your language. We don't talk about Bemidji around here."

"Do they have a Paul Bunyan celebration, too?" she asked. Mother said yes, but not as good as ours.

In that Jean Arthur voice again: "Did you say down south?"

Mother laughed. "Well, it is south," she said. "Everything's south. Bemidji's about 100 miles away. Always has been bad blood between the Falls and Bemidji. Every winter we read in the Minneapolis papers how cold it is in Bemidji. Propaganda from their Chamber of Commerce! *We're* the people with the cold weather!"

"How about some apple pie," she ordered. "Coffee too. That's all." Mother asked if she wanted it *à la mode*.

"What's *à la mode*?" With ice cream, mother said.

No, Jean Arthur said, but thanks. Again, that voice in A flat. Mother brought the pie and coffee, and sat down again. "You from around here?"

"No. I'm a Texas gal. I'm a writer, here to do a story about your Paul Bunyan Festival. Staying at the Koochiching Hotel there, across the street."

They settled down, the way women do, and started to talk. How cold does it get, Jean Arthur asked. So cold, mother replied, if you throw boiling water out the door in the wintertime, it freezes before it hits the ground and the ice will still be warm. They laughed. Jean Arthur said that where she's from it gets so dry in the summer that you can tell when fish are coming down the Rio Grande by the cloud of dust they raise. More laughter.

Jean Arthur complimented the pie. Mother invited her to the bake sale, raising money for the church furnace. I coughed. "Charlie, come out here," mother said. "Meet this lady from Texas!"

I came, held out my hand, looked up, and beheld not Jean Arthur, but Rita Hayworth.

She wasn't as skinny as Rita, but bigger, sort of more filled out. She was tall, about six feet, had long, flowing red hair, red lips, a heavy black wool dress, black cowboy boots, dangly gold earrings, and—wow—perfume. Something, though, was wrong with her face. There was a red scar on it that ran down her right cheek and over her chin, disappearing somewhere inside her dress. When she smiled, she smiled just a bit crooked.

"Hello, Charlie," she said, bending over at close range, "put 'er there!" We shook hands. "Name's Nelson. Mrs. Nelson." That handshake, as it turned out, was the start of my first love affair.

"I had a little boy like you, once," she said. "Let me scratch your head. Kids and dogs like to be scratched." She proceeded to scratch, and I tell you when I felt those fingernails digging into my scalp, something brand new and unprecedented went zapping through my nervous system.

You in the Boy Scouts, she asked. No, Cub Scouts, I stammered. Mother came to my rescue. "Tell her about your science project," she said. "Charlie goes out and looks at planets with Dad's big German telescope. Dad got it from the wreck of an observation balloon in the war."

"Will you teach me about stars and planets, Charlie?" Rita Hayworth asked. Sure he will, said mother. He'll show you the star maps he made for the Cub Scouts project.

The next evening we went over to the city ballpark to look at the stars. Rita carried the telescope; I carried the tripod and my star maps. We climbed into the top bleachers and set up the equipment. I found

Cassiopeia, Taurus the Bull, the Pleiades, Polaris, and *voilà*! Venus hanging like a lantern in the western sky. Then I lowered the scope and we watched men working on papermaking machines in the mill. We looked north across the river and watched the Fort Frances city band at its weekly practice in their city hall.

On the way back, she held my hand. Next day I had a pretty hard time keeping my mind on my lessons. All I could think about was that great, big, wonderful Rita Hayworth creation with her red hair and those fingernails making my ganglia twang.

Already this woman with the big raccoon coat had been noticed by several young men about town.

In wintertime in the Falls, women wear men's clothes—pants, boots, jackets, parkas, heavy mitts. Though it was spring, most of them hadn't switched yet. Mrs. Nelson was different. Every morning she walked down Third Street in that big raccoon coat, red hair flying in the wind, to the First National Bank, then the post office, and then to our restaurant for breakfast. Many eyes, in particular the eyes of young bachelors, followed her as she made her daily pilgrimage. She carried her head high, looked straight ahead, and wore a sort of a tight, crooked half-smile as if to say, "I know you're looking at me. Well, here I am. Take another look!" Nothing like Mrs. Nelson had been seen in our town for a long, long time.

Over the next few days, mother and Mrs. Nelson

got to be pretty good friends. Mother tried to get her to come to talk to the church ladies, but she declined. Word spread that this phenomenon from Texas was a writer who came to cover our Paul Bunyan Festival. Soon, though, young men and some older men, too, began to speculate. "She's a writer?" they'd say. "I don't see her interviewing people, taking pictures. What's a writer doing at the Koochiching Hotel? That's where lumberjacks rent rooms when they come to town."

Mother gently advised Mrs. Nelson to move to the Rex Hotel, a more appropriate place for a single woman. No, Mrs. Nelson said, the Koochiching's fine with me.

As I mentioned, we lived on the first floor of one of the tallest buildings in town. None of the upper-floor rooms were inhabited; they were used for storage or left vacant. Over the years I had explored the whole building. I had even climbed a ladder and pushed my way through a trapdoor to the fifth floor. There I found a small space just under the eaves with a venti-lator—just an opening with wooden slats—looking out upon the town. Bats were there, lots of them, clinging upside-down to the ridgepole on the ceiling, dropping every now and then to fly outside through a broken slat to the outside world.

This space became my own secret hideaway. I liked to lug Dad's telescope up the ladder to my hide-away and stick the scope's barrel out through a hole in the ventilator, just to see what I could see. The bats were nervous about this. I think they were disturbed when they saw my telescope narrowing their exit into the world out there.

On this beautiful spring day, I could see forever! To the east on Rainy Lake, ice was breaking up and there were patches of open water. Across the river in Canada, a black-haired teacher was writing words on a chalkboard. North into Ontario were farmhouses and unpainted gray barns. Above the dam in the Rainy River, Adolph McKinley was using a long pole to shepherd logs of white pine onto an endless chain into the mill. I watched people eating breakfast. I watched Mr. Murphy, our town's sole mail carrier, sorting letters on his kitchen table. I watched workers struggling to remove a huge wheel from a truck. I returned to watch Mr. Murphy sorting mail, opening some of the letters. I thought that was a bit strange.

I turned the telescope, sharply depressing its long barrel, and examined the Koochiching Hotel. Shades were pulled on most of the windows, but some had curtains that covered only the lower half. From my high angle I looked down into a bleak and barren room with a beat-up dresser, broken mirror, two wooden chairs, a calendar on the wall advertising Lifebuoy Soap, a brass hall-tree, and one bare electric light hanging from the ceiling. Something was moving on the bed. People. Looked like they were wrestling.

Wait a minute! Hold on! That's not wrestling! Whatever they're doing, it's not wrestling!

54

You could have hung a hat on my eyeballs as I watched what was happening on that bed. Two people, naked, were lying there, all tangled up, and one of them was Mrs. Nelson. No question about it. There was that red hair, there was the scar. I had wondered how far down it went. Now I knew. It continued down her neck and ended in the middle of her left breast.

I am not going to give you a cheap thrill by describing what I saw. You know what I saw. You know what they were doing. The whole world knows what they were doing. To me, though, it was a revelation. I watched with terrible fascination, my eyes glued to the scope, and as I watched I experienced a rush of very strong feelings, which included, but were not limited to, intense curiosity, nausea, and one or two miscellaneous sensations I had never felt before.

My whole moral structure came crashing down to earth. I kept talking to myself as I watched, "By golly, they really *do* do it. Really *do* do it. Oscar, guess you were right. Oscar, you were right!"

But why? Why do they do it? It didn't look like fun to me. They didn't laugh. There was something wrong with their smiles. Their smiles were wrong! When people talk to friends, you know, they bob their heads up and down, move their arms and hands, raise and lower their eyebrows, turn the corners of their mouths upward, and move their eyes around. Well, that's not what these two people on the bed were doing. Mrs. Nelson's smile was fixed and unchanging, a steady, crooked grimace painted on a mask. The men (I watched three more episodes) had what I'd call a leer—a fixed, straight-ahead, greedy, ugly look. They all were wearing masks! I tell you, there was something weird and primeval about it all.

My left arm felt paralyzed from holding the heavy telescope, but if it had fallen off I wouldn't have cared. A lumberjack, principal player in the second episode, was just leaving. She let him out, hooked the door chain, put on her bathrobe, got a key out of a glass on the window-ledge, fetched a metal box from under the bed, opened it, carefully placed some money inside, locked it, and returned the key to the glass.

She made a cup of coffee, sat again, then suddenly looked up as if she heard a knock on the door. She opened the door a crack, released the chain, and who walked in but Hugo Schlampp, the teller at the bank, the man who passed the collection plate every Sunday at our church, Schlampp of the two-toned shoes, with his tricky Clark Gable mustache. I watched him perform.

After Schlampp, another knock on the door and in walked Mr. Murphy, our genial bachelor mailman. He was fat, not lean and muscular like the first two. And I watched Mr. Murphy do his thing.

I couldn't eat, couldn't sleep, couldn't think as I tried to sort out everything I had seen. Who could I talk to? Why was Mrs. Nelson doing this?

I couldn't face her when she showed up the next

morning for breakfast. I was out in back, doing kitchen work. When I heard her voice I bugged out and went to my room. I was embarrassed, puzzled, alienated, hurt by what I had seen. I may have lost my appetite and lost sleep, but after she left our restaurant, I made a beeline to my sanctorum to catch the early morning show in the Koochiching hotel.

The word somehow was out among the town's young bachelors: the red-haired phenomenon was not a writer for the *Saturday Evening Post*. She was a hooker, doing business at the Koochiching. Maybe it was Hugo Schlampp, our plastic Clark Gable, who leaked it to his bachelor friends.

Her routine was always the same: breakfast at our place, to the bank, then back for business. In a morning, she would perform four or five times, first collecting the money at the door. At noon she cooked her meal on a hot plate, washed and dried the dishes, took a nap, and then back to business again. I was able to examine her room in great detail. The roots of her red hair were black.

Mrs. Nelson's rate (I could actually focus on the presidents' faces on the currency) was five dollars per trick. As the festival approached—only one day to go— she raised her price to seven-fifty and later the same day to ten. In the three days before our festival had started, I watched a total of twenty-three episodes. I was getting a bit bored.

Most of her clients were lumberjacks. Some,

though, were men I recognized: Schlampp, of course, from the bank; Mortimer Dewey, our high school football coach; and Mr. Murphy. It seemed that after a performance, our postman always wanted to stick around and talk. I watched him unfolding what looked like a map. They discussed it over coffee.

And then our long-awaited day was here, our liberation, our glorious rite of spring, our own Paul Bunyan Festival. The weather that morning, everyone agreed, was a bit "nippy."

About 7:30 that Saturday morning, the MD&W passenger train—MD&W stood for Minnesota, Dakota, and Western railroad—pulled in and unloaded about 100 sleep-deprived human beings, big-city people who had come to see our festival.

Beer joints on Third Street at 8:30 in the morning already were jammed. From my perch I concentrated on morning gymnastics in Mrs. Nelson's room. By 9:30 a.m. she had accomplished the whole percussion section of the Fort Frances Band, which had come across the river to be in our festival parade. The Canadian musicians took their instruments (no pun intended) right into the room with them. I saw it all.

The Falls City Band, the Fort Frances Band, and our high school marching band all proceeded to line up over on Second Street. At union headquarters, workers gathered, listened to instructions, and tapped a keg just to get started. Automobiles from distant locations—Chevys, Dodges, Ford V-8s, Oakland roadsters with rumble seats—piled into town. A bus arrived containing a drum-and-bugle corps from Ely, followed by the Fort William Bagpipe Band and a cavalcade of blue-uniformed American Legion veterans from Bemidji. Professional ax-throwers, log-rollers, sawyers, folk-tune fiddlers, and tall-tale tellers got ready to compete for prize money.

The big parade was scheduled to start at 10:00 a.m. From my perch I watched the festival take shape. Crowds were starting to line Third Street for several blocks. Old people were being pushed to the curbs in wheelchairs. Policemen already were working hard to keep people on the sidewalk, off the street. A line of "queen candidates" from Duluth, Hibbing, and Virginia, some sitting in horse-drawn carriages, others propped up on fire trucks, took shape. Bagpipers from Fort William formed a circle, skirling, warming up. Our mayor and Fort Frances's mayor sat happily side-by-side in an open convertible. Hugh McCostley, about seven feet tall and made taller with four-inch spikes on his boots and a tall Scotch cap; was ready to lead the parade as Paul Bunyan himself.

I swung the telescope to the north and witnessed the traditional ceremony at the bridge. World War I veterans from both countries met at the center, stopped, saluted, and marched back. Boom went the cannon, starting things off.

Now, the month of May in my town was always thought to be a pretty safe month to plan outdoor activities. May is the month of transformation. People themselves have been transformed. Gardeners talk about plans for their vegetable gardens. Men get fishing tackle out and make bets on when that old Model A is going to go through the ice on Rainy Lake. Young men's fancies turn to thoughts of love.

From my perch, I watched the parade start to move, Hugh McCostley at its head. Something, though, was wrong. The bats had been bothering me all day, dropping from their spots on the ridge-pole, nervously flying outside past my left ear, and quickly returning. They were uneasy about something.

And now, over on Second Street, musicians' hats were being blown off. Pieces of paper and other stuff swirled around. Below on Third Street spectators along the parade route were leaving, walking, some running, back to their parked cars. I watched the canvas awning for the King Joy Café come crashing down on some people on the sidewalk. I heard faint shouts and screams.

I pointed my telescope up north into Canada and saw what had concerned the bats. About fifty or sixty miles away, an enormous black cloud loomed high in the air. Little bursts of lightning flashed through the black mass, which rested on a sort of thick, white base close to the ground. I focused on that white layer and found that it was a tangled, swirling web of snow. I watched an old Model T Ford coming south down a gravel road, apparently trying to outrun the storm.

The white web caught up with the car, engulfed it, and continued in my direction. Our old wooden building began to creak and groan. The bats were now perfectly still, hunkered upside-down on the ridgepole, waiting. The floor moved just a bit under my feet. I knew it was time to go, but not without one last look at the Koochiching.

I checked. Someone was beating the hell out of Mrs. Nelson.

She was naked, he was naked, and he was slapping her around the room—some lumberjack. She was covered in blood, holding her face with her hands.

I half-stumbled, half-fell down the swaying ladder, and then came crashing down the steps, one floor, two floors, three. I grabbed the telephone, dialed zero, and shouted, "They're killing Mrs. Nelson. Killing her!"

"Who are you?" the operator asked. I couldn't even remember my name.

"Get police!" I screamed. "Mrs. Nelson! Second floor, Koochiching Hotel! He's killing her!"

My parents were out, watching the parade somewhere. I grabbed my parka, raced outside, and turned on Third Street, fighting the wind. Garbage cans, shingles, pieces of wood, pieces of glass, wreckage of the parade were flying all over the place. It had become very dark, almost pitch black. People were running pell-mell for safety. Some took refuge in Pearson's Bakery, the City Drug store, or in one of the beer joints.

Confessions of a Jackpine Savage

Sharp pellets of snow were coming in straight, not down, but straight into our faces.

Two kilted bagpipers were trying to pull their bass drum out of the Bon Ton Café's front window, which had been smashed. A horse lay on its back, kicking wildly amid a welter of reins and a broken single-tree. A patrol car drove up and down the street with a policeman on the running board shouting, "Take cover! Do not go home! Take cover!"

By the time I got to the Koochiching, some men were carrying Mrs. Nelson out on a stretcher. I watched them fight against the blizzard to load her into an ambulance. Then I ran into the hotel, up the stairs to the second floor, and down the hall to her room.

I pulled the black box out from under her bed, took the key from the water glass, and was all set to leave when I heard someone at the door. Hugging the box, I ducked into the coat-closet, hunched down behind Mrs. Nelson's big raccoon coat, and talked seriously to Jesus.

Now let me pause to tell you something important about prayers. Some of them go right through, some don't. Most of the blessings we automatically recite at mealtime never leave the house. Words without thoughts never go to heaven. But the prayer I offered from the bottom of that closet, that prayer, I tell you, went to heaven with a great big stamp on it that said "Top Priority!"

Someone was standing just outside the closet.

I saw his two-toned shoes. Hugo Schlampp!

He was there for the same reason I was: the black box. The shoes didn't move. He was wondering if he should search the closet. Then the shoes moved on. I wet my pants. He left the room.

I waited a few minutes, then grabbed Mrs. Nelson's big fur coat, rolled it around the box, and raced down the hall to the fire-escape ladder. Out into the blackness I went, into the worst blizzard in Koochiching County's history. It was a job getting down that ladder with my bundle, fingers freezing, eyes squinted shut against the sharp snow. I guess that prayer was still on duty, because I made it to the street, and there was a fire truck loaded with people. As it started to move, I hitched a ride on the rear, and held on all the way to the hospital; the longest half mile ride of my life.

My fingers were so cold I nearly couldn't unclench them when it came time to get off of the fire truck. Somehow I did. I stumbled into the hospital and wandered around until I found a receiving room. There she was, lying on a stretcher, eyes closed.

"What're you doing here?" a big white nurse said, advancing.

"She's my MOTHER! She's my MOTHER!" I screamed. The nurse shrugged and disappeared.

They were bringing more stretchers in and lining them up in the hallway. I stood by Mrs. Nelson. She opened her eyes.

"Good . . . Cub . . . Scout," she said in a faint whisper through blue and swollen lips. She closed her eyes for a long time. Then I took the black box and placed it under her hand. She opened her eyes. "You got it . . ." she whispered. Crooked smile. I handed her the key. "How . . . ?"

I then told her about my hideout on our fifth floor, and my father's telescope. Told her I had watched what she was doing.

She didn't say anything for a long time. I held her hand. "Tough way . . . make a living, Charlie," she said, eyes still closed.

I told her that I saw her get hurt.

"Men . . ." she whispered. "One way or another . . . they . . . have to . . . do it . . . but . . . don't you do it . . . that way, Charlie."

I told her how I hid when Hugo Schlampp came in, and prayed. I told her how my prayer had worked.

She handed me the key. "Open the box."

I did so. Struggling to raise herself, she removed a fistful of bills from the box and handed them to me. "Tell . . . your mother . . . for her church." Then she lay back and closed her eyes, and slept, a trace of that crooked smile still on her face.

Out again into the storm I went. This time the sixty-mile-per-hour wind was at my back. Mother was not home, but out, helping someone. In my room, the door pulled shut, I counted the money Mrs. Nelson had given me. The total came to $735.

Sunday morning dawned bright, clear, and cold. The blizzard had left snowdrifts three or four feet deep. We had a minus-twenty-five-degree temperature and a dazzling universe under a cloudless pale-blue sky. The Highway Patrol had closed both highways out of town. About noon, the MD&W wheezed in, over three hours late, its cowcatcher and engine one huge, white block of snow. By mid-afternoon snowplows had cleared Third Street, but it was a few days before all streets were open again.

The amazing thing was the way the people of my town reacted to the worst winter storm in Koochiching County's history.

The day after, bright and early, they grabbed shovels, any kind of shovel, and went to work digging out driveways and sidewalks, shouting, laughing, passing along information they had heard on the radio, joking about the "brass monkey" weather, working together, helping each other.

Without any instructions or emergency plan, telephone operators called shut-ins. "Dr. Comstock: We have people coming over to shovel you out. They need you at the hospital."

"Mrs. Pavek: Your daughter stayed overnight at her uncle's house. Don't worry."

"Has anybody checked on Mr. Lundgren, that old bachelor farmer all alone at his place on the Reserve Road?"

That was well and good, but what should I do with

65

all that money? Mrs. Nelson said it was for my church. And wouldn't you know, services were held as usual. God doesn't take a snow day. Mother and I bundled up and trudged the few blocks to church. As we made our way through the drifts, I wanted to talk to Mother about it, ask her for her good advice, but I couldn't. Too much to explain. So that morning, when Hugo Schlampp sent the collection plate down our pew, I dropped my hymnal on the floor to distract Mother. As she bent to reach for it, I slipped in the roll of bills, and passed the plate along.

When the hymn ended, I turned to watch Schlampp and the other ushers gather at the rear of the church, making a quick survey of the day's gifts. The ushers stood with mouths agape while Schlampp unrolled my bundle. With a feeling of inexpressible joy I witnessed his frustration. The bank teller knew there's only one person—one woman—in town with that many fifty-dollar bills.

When Mother and I left I made a point of passing Schlampp, and giving him my brightest smile. "It was from Mrs. Nelson," I murmured sweetly.

For four days after school I went back to the hospital to see her. On the fifth day she was not there. Apparently she had paid her hospital bill, slipped out, raccoon coat, black box and all, and caught the early bus to Minneapolis.

It turned out that Mr. Murphy, our affable mail carrier, disappeared on that same day. A man wearing a Stetson hat had come to town to find out who was intercepting and forging veterans' checks. He arrived just a few hours too late. Mr. Murphy had flown the coop. Somebody must have tipped him off. When I had watched Mr. Murphy organizing those letters on his kitchen table, I thought he was doing his duty. He actually was actually locating veterans' checks, forging signatures, and cashing them at the bank in Littlefork, twenty-five miles away. Nobody ever heard from Murphy again. Nobody heard about Mrs. Nelson, either. But I learned some years later where they were.

I was in the U.S. Army stationed in Adak, in the Aleutian Islands. One day I was killing time in a USO Quonset hut, just leafing a *Life Magazine*, when a picture caught my eye. It was a photo of people waiting to catch a bus, sitting on a long bench in San Jose, Costa Rica. They looked familiar. I asked the USO attendant for a magnifying glass, to get a better look.

There she was, my first love, sitting on that bench in San Jose. It was Mrs. Nelson, all right, and sitting beside her was—guess who—our long-gone postman, Mr. Murphy. Both of them were dressed like locals. Mr. Murphy now flaunted a big black mustache. Mrs. Nelson's Rita Hayworth hair was now jet black. There was that long red scar on her cheek. I suppose I could have notified the postal authorities to bring Murphy to justice, but I decided just to let things be.

The Tuba and Its Uses In Community Development

We tuba players know we're special. Ask us and we'll tell you straight-out: "Special? You bet! Without us, all those others would just be dancing around aimlessly up there. We're fundamental. We bring music down to earth! We're the anchors."

But my tuba was more than an anchor. It was a weapon of justice.

It all started sophomore year, during the weekly practice of our high school orchestra in International Falls, Minnesota. We'd been working on a piece from *Tristan and Isolde* for our spring concert. One passage required me—the only tuba player in the orchestra, we didn't have any string basses—to blow a fundamental tone in lower E-flat and hold it for twelve or fourteen slow beats. That's a long time for a tuba player to hold a note.

At this particular after-school practice we were murdering Tristan again, and again I took a big gulp of air and started to hold that long E-flat. As I did so, I was absent-mindedly speculating about the mammary charms of Miss Jensen, our director. She had, I tell you, a most spectacular set of breastworks. Thinking out loud, as they say, I spoke into the tuba's mouthpiece. "Twin beauts! Twin beauts! Oh, look at those twin beauts!"

Eddie Halvorson over in percussion started to laugh uncontrollably, all doubled-over, practically rolling on the floor. He had heard my comment! His job was to keep a steady beat, but of course the beat got all fouled up. Miss Jensen stopped the music, glared at Eddie, smiled at me, and we started once again to dismember Tristan.

That was my first discovery: not only could I make tuba words, but I could aim them, project them out into the waiting world.

It was our secret, Eddie's and mine. People over in strings, brass, and woodwinds couldn't hear my words over the sounds they themselves were making. I gossiped with Eddie, but only occasionally, about Miss Jensen's mammary charms. I'd aim, blow, and talk over Eddie's way and watch him double up with laughter. What fun!

A few years later while home on break from the U, I made another discovery with the tuba. I could make a bathtub talk.

My father had a heavy Conn "double B" tuba that he played in our city band. It weighed about fifty pounds and had a wonderful, deep, velvet tone. Those deep, rich tones from father's horn often were the sound that woke us up in the morning. Almost every day before work he'd go into basement and "blow a few long tones to keep my chops in shape."

I noticed that when father played those morning serenades, certain glasses, bowls, and other pieces of glassware in our kitchen responded in the same tone. It seemed as if they were coupling, reaching out, mating with their own special vibration. B flat from the basement always resonated with our empty fish bowl. F sharp always rattled a piece of loose glass in our kitchen window. Bass strings in our old piano vibrated softly to Father's serenades. B flat from the tuba brought a resonant response from our upstairs bathtub. A big B-flat in the basement made the whole house vibrate.

On the west side of our house we were blessed with what we called Paranoia Acres. Two ancient dog-breeders lived there. Their house was always dark—they never came out into the light of day. They had five huge Dobermans that barked and barked and barked all the time. The dogs patrolled around the house on a well-worn trail. Nobody dared go into their yard. I witnessed a substitute postman learn his lesson one day, entering Paranoia Acres through the gate. He was immediately thrown flat on his back by two huge dogs that pinned him to the ground. Ten thousand letters and papers went flying through the air. From that day on, he did what the regular postman did: Bundled the mail and stuck it through one of the interstices in the fence.

Early every evening, from about eight until ten, those dogs would howl. Then they'd retire for the night. I thought: "Could I *make* those dogs howl?"

Second question: "Would Paranoia's bathtub vibrate, too?"

The window on my second-floor bedroom faced Paranoia's upper bathroom, and the window was always open. One happy June night, about 10:00 p.m.—both my parents were in bed—I retrieved my father's tuba, waited for Paranoia's lights to go out, and then blew a soft, low E-flat out their way. No response. I tried B flat. Again, no response. I tried A flat, and bingo! I got a warm and satisfying response. Their bathtub was tuned in A flat!

Each evening, about ten o'clock, after the Para-noids had gone to bed, I aimed and blew a soft A-flat through their bathroom window. The bathtub responded, and the dogs did, too, offering a veritable chorus of howls. These were different kinds of howls: higher and interspersed with short, sharp barks.

Lights went on. I put my tuba down. The howling stopped. I waited ten, twelve minutes, and then fired another A flat across the way. Lights would go on! Dogs would howl! I'd wait until they went out, and then blow another A flat. I kept this up every night for about two weeks.

Neighbors, lots of them, complained. Police came to investigate. After three weeks of these canine choruses, a delegation of neighbors went to a city council meeting and raised hell. The Paranoids then decided to move. A hard-working Vietnamese family bought their house.

I turned my attention to a different kind of problem: traffic jams caused by spiritualists on the other side of our house.

Our spiritualist neighbors were running a retail business in direct violation of our village's zoning laws. Cars were always parked in front of their house and down the street, sometimes blocking neighbors' driveways. We never saw the owners in the light of day—they never came over to say "good morning" or to apologize for the chaos they were causing.

Spiritualists from a wide area convened here by day and by night. From our second-story hallway window, using my father's binoculars, I could see groups of ten to twelve people sitting in a circle, raising their hands as if they were singing or calling, colored lights moving slowly around the room.

One summer evening—both my parents were at a meeting—I set up the tuba facing the spiritualists' half-open bathroom window, took aim, and blew a few experimental tones searching for the natural frequency of the bathtub. Nothing happened until I blew a soft B-flat. Touchdown! Spiritualism in B flat!

I waited until a guest came in, turned on the

light, and prepared to use the bathroom. Then, speaking softly but distinctly in B flat, I spoke these magic words: "You . . . farted . . . during . . . the séance . . . Farts . . . interfere . . . with . . . celestial energy . . . Please do . . . not . . . fart . . . again . . . during a . . . séance."

These words produced a swift reaction. With my binoculars focused through certain slits and interstices in the window shades, laughing until tears ran down my nose, I could see people waving their arms, shouting, denying fart accusations, walking out the door, driving away.

It was so much fun, in fact, that I spread it out over two months' time. Once a week I'd deliver my fart routine and watch with satisfaction as clients left, never to return. Fewer and fewer cars were parked along the street, there were fewer traffic jams. Soon no cars were parked there anymore. One day the séance people pulled up stakes: sold their house, and moved away.

One last time I used my father's tuba to bring sweet serenity to our neighborhood. This one was easy.

A very loud heavy metal band practiced three times a week just across the street. Their loud, whanging sounds could be heard a quarter-mile away. Whenever I heard them tuning up, I'd fetch our tuba, wait for the maniacs to start, take aim, and blow a few random notes their way, but in a different rhythm.

The mixture caused chaos. The metal band, like the others, sold out and moved on. More civilized people moved in.

After I graduated I established a business based on my discoveries.

Our major product is simply a huge warning device—a giant talking tuba, if you will—that brings words-on-tones to citizens in a metropolitan area. Most American cities now have purchased and are using my device. It has saved many lives. For instance, its voice might say "TORNADO! Suburbs to the east, TAKE COVER! Other areas, stay alert!" At Christmastime—despite the ACLU—it will say "Merry Christmas" to one and all. On Election Day it reminds citizens, "It's your duty to vote today!"

We also make an automobile horn. One light tap evokes courteous phrases in traffic like "Please sir (or madam)," "Thank you for letting me in," and "I'm about to exit." A forceful punch brings "No texting, you idiot," or "Off with that damned cell phone." A device mounted on the rear bumper will, when the driver presses a button, say, "Back off, you stupid ass."

MORNING PARADE

We were having breakfast, my wife Margaret and I. It was very early in the morning, still dark outside, Memorial Day.

"Lousy time to have a parade," I said. "Parades should be in the sun, in the daylight."

"I asked that new couple to join us," said Margaret. "Those Alvarez people. They got an invitation this year."

Pretty young for this parade. Afghanistan, I figured. Maybe Iraq.

"Strange parade," I said, and once again, "strange parade. Always just a few people in the parade. Always just a few people who get invited."

The doorbell rang. Margaret left, returning with Ricardo and Miranda Alvarez. There was general smiling, nice words, handshakes.

"We're a bit early. How about a cup of coffee?" I poured and Margaret put out a few doughnuts. Ricardo, it turned out, was an automobile mechanic; Miranda, a nurse's assistant. They had emigrated from Santo Domingo, about a decade ago. We schmoozed a bit. Great baseball players come from Santo Domingo, I said.

The four of us walked the few blocks to the parade

route, carrying our light folding chairs. Dim figures stood along the darkened street, talking quietly. Every now and then somebody would step off the curb and peer west, down the street. There was no laughter, no neighbor-to-neighbor talk. We set up our chairs on the grassy lawn between the sidewalk and the curb and waited. "Wish I'd brought a sweater," Margaret said. A siren wailed far away, taking somebody to the hospital.

The first signs of morning were now etched on some low, red clouds on the eastern horizon. I stepped from the curb and looked west down the street. Something moved, a lone figure coming our way, around the corner. "I think they're coming," I whispered.

We all rose from our chairs.

A pale young man in a faded army uniform appeared under the streetlight, walking slowly, almost casually, pausing occasionally to look up at the sky. He carried a rifle in his left hand, barrel pointed downward. He was bareheaded and carried a helmet in his right hand. Although he walked close to the spectators at the curb, he showed no sign of recognition, no smile, no "good morning," and moved on. There was no sound.

"So young," Margaret whispered. "Just a high school kid."

A group of soldiers and sailors, about twenty-five or thirty, now entered the circle under the streetlight. The soldiers carried rifles. Two young women in uniforms with red crosses on armbands passed by, chatting silently. An older naval officer with four gold stripes on his sleeves passed. "Captain," I whispered. "Probably got torpedoed and went down with his ship." Four sailors appeared, soundlessly talking and laughing. They wore bleached dungarees, short-sleeved shirts, and white caps stuck to the back of their heads. Then six young men in heavy sheepskin jackets walked by. "Looks like a crew from a B-17," I said. "All went down together."

The parade passed in utter silence: no drums, no sergeant calling cadence, not even the scraping of boots on the concrete. On the branch of a maple tree above the street a robin suddenly broke forth with its throaty morning birdsong. One of the soldiers turned his head, looked up, smiled, and pointed with his thumb toward the robin, apparently making a comment to a comrade by his side. They appeared to laugh, but there was no sound of laughter.

The morning sun now broke over the horizon, flooding the street with golden light. One soldier stopped, raised both arms stiffly toward the sun, threw his head back, and opened his mouth as if he was singing a morning paean to the sun.

"I think I see him!" Ricardo whispered, pointing. "The one in the middle—our son!" The young man carried a rifle. He appeared to be talking, smiling, perhaps telling a joke.

Miranda, too, had spotted their son, and

suddenly there was an ear-piercing scream about ten inches from my ear. "Ay Dio, Dio, Dio!" she screamed. "Regreso hijo mio! Regreso! Regreso!" Oh God, God, God! Come back, come back to me!

Miranda broke from the group and ran into the street toward the soldiers. Ricardo and I rushed out, seized her, and hauled her back. She struggled furiously, slipped, fell to her hands and knees, slowly sagged, and lay flat on the grassy strip, crying and talking incoherently. Her husband, also crying, knelt down and vainly tried to calm her. A small crowd collected. Someone appeared with a glass of water.

The parade turned the corner and was gone. Ricardo took a light sweater he had been wearing and put it around his wife's shoulders. The four of us walked silently to the Alvarez's house.

Back home at our kitchen table: silence, wide, long, and deep.

"I think I saw my brother," I finally said. "He was over on the far side, in a group."

Margaret rose from the table and walked to the window.

"They seemed so happy," she said. "They were laughing! Did you see the way that soldier looked when he heard the robin? Like it was the first bird he'd ever seen. And that soldier who held out his arms? Just like he was embracing the sun!"

"They don't have much to be happy about," I said.

"Maybe they were happy to breathe that sweet

morning air," she said. "Maybe they were happy to feel the warmth of the sun, happy to be walking and laughing and joking with their buddies. Maybe they were happy to be alive again, even if it was just for one morning parade."

ARTISTIC CRITICISM
AND THE DEVIL

The devil came to see me, oozing out from under my refrigerator about ten o'clock in the morning on a cold winter day in 1980. I'm a writer. I had seen the devil before.

He could have knocked, but that's the way he enters my house: a dark green blob on my kitchen floor that takes shape as an ugly little monster about two feet high, horns, tail, and all, skin a sickly dark magenta. Magenta, you know, is the color you get if you pour blood on a bright-blue fabric. The devil's own color.

I was glad to see him again. I needed advice.

"Help me up," he said. No "good morning," no apology, just: "Help me up."

I bent over to lift him but couldn't find a place to grab because of the sharp protuberances on his thick, warty skin.

"Under my arms," he said in his raspy, high-pitched voice, "Grab under my arms!" He turned around. I lifted and placed him on the kitchen table. His legs and his tail dangled over the edge. He was heavy, about forty pounds, I'd estimate.

He helped himself to a shluck of my coffee. "I hear you want to be a music critic," he said. That's right, I replied. I would like to be a music critic. "You might actually make it," he said. "You were a C-plus musician, you're a half-assed writer, and you've got perfect pitch. That's a *big* advantage. Music critics like to *pretend* they have perfect pitch, like to pretend they hear sopranos' off-key notes way up there. You can actually hear wrong tones, even in the second violins."

I thanked him for the compliment. As always, he knew everything about me. I knew you were active in other forms of journalism, I said, but what is your connection to music and art criticism?

He seemed to be offended. "Artistic criticism," he said shrilly. "Artistic criticism is my exclusive domain! I'm in charge of all of it, ALL artistic criticism!"

He dipped a bony finger into my coffee, stuck his wet finger in my sugar bowl, sucked his finger, looked up, and smiled. He had a bewitching smile, that dirty, deceptive little dwarf. Changeable, too: big screaming fit followed by that cute little smile. "Let's get a couple of things straight," he said. "Now, in terms that you will understand: You will be a cub reporter and I will be your editor. You will be reporting to me."

This, of course, was pretty hard for me to take. At the same time, he had given me good advice in the past, so I held my temper. "All right," he said, "Let's

84

get going. You wrote something for *Allegro*." Yes, I responded. *Allegro* used to be the premier art connoisseur's magazine, published in fourteen languages.

"Well," he said, sticking his finger into my sugar bowl again, "let's take a look at your review. This is going to be your first lesson."

I got up, went to my desk, fetched the story—a review of a concert by the Welsh Singers—returned, and handed it to him. It took him about five minutes to read my piece. From time to time he chuckled and made sarcastic *sotto voce* comments like, "Oh no!"

"Not bad, but tear it up," he said, finally. I gently pointed out that I had invested fifteen to twenty hours in the piece.

"No. Tear it up," he said, standing on the table, stubby little tail flicking sugar all over the place. "It's fundamentally *wrong, wrong, WRONG!* You've violated the First Rule of Artistic Criticism: *Never use the first person.* You've violated the second one, too: *Never use the active voice.* Always use the passive voice! Never write: *I maintain*; always, *it could be maintained* or *arguably it can be maintained.* Give your reader the idea—and do it grammatically—that your judgment is the will of the artistic community, the general consensus of people better-qualified, more intelligent, more gifted than the reader, that dumb peasant slave. Always be indirect: passive voice! No first person!"

A tiny buzzer went off: his pager. "Got to go," he said. "Next lesson: here, one week from today, same time!" I helped him down and watched him deflate and flow back under the refrigerator. Then I rewrote that first story about the Welsh Singers and sent it to *Allegro*. It clicked! I was on my way as a critic.

The devil and I continued to meet every week for about six months, each time covering another aspect of indirect speech. He taught me how to use sentence adverbs such as *happily* and *regretfully* (but never *hopefully*); how to give, deceptively, the impression that I had heard the singer or organization perform before; and, of course, how to pepper my copy with snotty little puns, double meanings, and French phrases in italics. In every review I followed an inflexible rule, complaining about flat tones. Whether I had heard them or not. The little monster left me with a small dictionary of haughty and devilish adjectives, which I found very useful.

I had a very satisfying career as a music critic. After twenty years in the pantheon, honored by all, I finally retired. As things turned out, in retirement I entered my own particular hell. Years of indirect speech had spoiled my *thinking*. I am not able to write a letter, a memo. I can't even *sign my own name* without trying to give it that indirect general feeling of universal consensus.

I can't *talk* anymore in a direct, subject-verb-object-of-the-verb way, like normal people do. If someone asks me, "Did you like the movie?" I say that I was *entertained*. If I am stopped by a traffic policeman, and opinions are exchanged, I say I believe he's *in error*. If a friend asks, "How are you?" I say that it seems, or appears, that I'm better. If I disagree with a person, I won't say, "I disagree," or "on the other hand." I start my dissent with *arguably*. In other social situations, I freely use sentence adverbs like *happily, unexpectedly, surprisingly*, or *partially*. My friends have fallen away. People may like to read what an art critic writes, but who wants to *listen* to one?

At any rate, a good time was had by all.

THE
INVENTOR'S
GURGLES

I was flattered the other day to get a call from an old classmate, Mercer Emerson. After school he went on to become a professor of linguistics. From what the newspapers said about him when he retired, he had become an important scholar in his field. I remember him as small, alert, fat, and very smart. He had a great memory.

"As I recall, you became an inventor," he said on the phone. "I've located something in which you may have a professional interest. Come on over. We'll sit on the balcony, drink a beer, talk a bit about old times, and I'll tell you what I found."

I readily accepted, and the next day drove across town to Mercer's building, took the elevator to the top floor, found his apartment, and met him and Evelyn, his young wife. Evelyn was slim, quite tall, and had flaxen-colored hair wrapped in a sort of bun at the back of her neck. *Probably one of his graduate students*, I thought. Emerson was still fat, still jovial. He seemed pleased to see me.

Evelyn smiled briefly as we shook hands, and that

was the only smile I got from her during my entire two-hour visit. "Something's wrong here," I thought. "Something's wrong."

Emerson, though, was the soul of hospitality. Evelyn helped him into his chair, went into the kitchen, and returned with beer, crackers, and cheese. Emerson poured. Evelyn took her seat about ten feet away, just out of our conversational orbit.

"Well, well," he intoned, "after all these years! And how has life treated you?" I said I lived an inventor's life, eking out a living, four or five patents, nothing spectacular.

From time to time I heard a cough from the sidelines, not the serious kind of cough when something sticks in the throat, but a soft cough that communicates a message. Each time Emerson would glance in his wife's direction, then continue in his affable way.

"The other day I went to an antique car show, and there was one of my old students, Alex Radetzky. He was at the center of a big crowd, showing off his 1922 Bentley—one of the world's rare automobiles. This Bentley, I tell you, was in perfect condition. Alex recognized me, came over, and we talked."

Another cough wafted our way. Emerson glanced toward his wife and continued, just a bit faster. "I was fascinated by that '22 Bentley. I said it must be worth half a million dollars. 'No,' Alex said. 'Two, maybe three million. Only five of these left in the whole world.'

"I was very curious," Emerson went on. "I asked

him right out where he got the money to buy a museum piece like that '22 Bentley. 'Last time I saw you,' I said, 'you were a bankrupt graduate student!' You know what he said? Don't laugh! He told me he made his money by inventing a drain for a commode that says, 'Wash your hands!'"

Evelyn stood up. "Remember, Emerson," she said, "we have that appointment." Her mouth was drawn in a single, straight line. He nodded, and continued with his story.

"Well, Alex told me that his luck changed when he moved into an apartment, a dismal rat-trap on the other side of town. He was really down on his luck. But when he took his first bath, just as the last water went down the drain, he heard a deep and gurgley voice say 'Auf Wiedersehen!' He couldn't believe his ears! The words in that little German greeting were clearly articulated. He ran more water into the tub, removed the plug, and there it came again, loud and clear: 'Auf Wiedersehen!' He filled and emptied the tub many times, and each time, as the last water was leaving, he got those same, two cheery words. You know, they mean a bit more than just 'goodbye.' More like 'see you soon,' or 'until the next time.'"

I stole a quick glance at Evelyn. She was standing now, looking over our heads, and the lids of her eyes had descended, forming tiny slits.

Emerson continued, rather quickly, "Well Alex was also an inventor, you know, so he tried to figure out what caused those words. Got a flashlight and shone it down into the drain. Nothing there but a big, black hole. But when he inserted his fingers into the drain and pressed them against the inner walls of the tube, bingo! The inner surface of the drain was covered with small protuberances of different shapes and sizes. Someone had painstakingly fashioned tiny blisters, ridges, and crevices so that water passing over them would gurgle and replicate human words!"

Evelyn strode into the kitchen, from which there came certain crashes and bangings.

"Well," Emerson said, now quite rapidly, "Alex discovered some small letters and figures pressed into the rim of the drain. They spelled the address of a firm in Germany, town near Frankfurt. He went to the phone, called Germany, managed to contact that same little factory. The Germans were very apologetic. The *Auf Wiedersehen* drains, they said, were intended only for the German market. Somehow, some had mistakenly been sent to America.

"Alex went over to Germany and stayed six months with that same German firm. Made a drain for the American market. Very ingenious: Press that little flush lever on your commode, and it will say 'Wash your hands, please!' That's where he made his money. Most hospitals in this country right now are using Alex's drains. Some day, he said, when every person in the U.S. flushes the toilet, he or she will hear 'Wash your hands!'"

Evelyn appeared carrying her coat, her purse, and a very tight lip. "I hate to break this up, Emerson, but we must go." She helped him to his feet.

I asked if I could get Alex Radetzky's telephone number. "I'll send it to you," Emerson said over his shoulder.

I drove straight home, my inventor's brain buzzing. Gurgles that talk! At first, the idea seemed ridiculous. A gurgle, after all, is a bundle of sound waves caused when water is poured on air. The air escapes in bubbles, the bubbles burst, and the sound resonates in the tube. But gurgles that make words?

The next day I called Emerson. Evelyn answered. "I'd like to get Alex Radetzky's telephone number," I said. "Can't find a listing."

"Oh," she said, "I'm so sorry, but I never got the chance to talk to you about Emerson. These days we have to take his stories with a grain of salt."

I was slow in getting the message. I asked again for Alex Radetzky's telephone number. "I'm sorry to tell you this," she said, "but there *isn't* any Alex Radetzky. There never was a graduate student with that name. There never was a commode that said '*Auf Wiedersehen*' or 'wash your hands.' Emerson's back to the hospital. I brought him there as soon as you left."

This was pretty hard for me to handle. No Alex Radetzky. No gurgled words. It was all a joke, all Emerson's imagination. I suppose I could have taken offense. Why did he go to the trouble of calling me, inviting me to his house, and telling me that story?

But I'm an inventor, and I can't get his crazy idea out of my head.

For years, as water from my bathtub goes down the drain, I have heard words, English words. His story started me thinking: Could we really manipulate a drain so it would say words, like "wash your hands" or "zip up your fly"? Emerson might be mentally ill, but his gurgles-that-talk idea came from a first-rate imagination.

I've been spending a lot of time in the bathroom lately, listening to sounds from my bathtub and commode and making a list. I've heard about 130 gurgle words, in English. The problem is, they're all nouns. Many of them end in-tion, for example: education, transportation, expiation. I keep believing that someone out there is trying to tell me something, but without verbs there's no meaning. Lots of nouns designating things out there but not one damned verb that tells what happens to those things. You've got to have verbs to make meaning.

I hate to give up on this. If I could get a commode to talk, there would be a big-big-big market for it. Maybe—crazy thought—maybe my bathtub drain was made in Germany. I can find no evidence—no engraved data on the drain. If it were made in Germany, though, that would explain things. All those wet-sounding German verbs would just be waiting. At the appropriate time they would all come out in one, big gurgley rush.

THE PROFESSOR
AND THE LETHAL
CLICHÉ

He was a retired teacher of English, very tall, neatly trimmed beard, always with a white shirt, always a bow tie. He lived by himself in a modest apartment, cooked his own meals, and kept to himself. His expression seemed to say that he was in some sort of stress: a toothache, perhaps, shoes that were too small, or gas trapped deep in his intestinal tract. He never married and had only one relative, a nephew, in California.

"Here he comes," people would say. "Watch your language, it's the professor!" His name was Martin. Professor Edward Martin.

For twenty years he taught English in our high school, and later at our community college. He taught grammar like a drill sergeant teaches recruits in boot camp.

"Good morning!" he'd shout, striding into the classroom.

We'd all shout, "Good morning!"

"Subjunctive?" he'd call.

"Contrary to fact!" we'd answer in unison.

"Four kinds of pronouns?"

"Personal, relative, interrogative, indefinite!" we'd scream.

"Supersede? Spell it!"

"S-U-P-E-R-S-E-D-E," we'd belt out, together.

"Pluperfect?"

"Action completed! Helping verb, past tense!"

"Inter and intra?"

"Between and within!"

"Super and supra?"

"Above and on top of!"

And so on, each day a different drill covering spelling, style, grammar, and punctuation. He made it very clear this drill had nothing to do with correctness, but everything to do with getting a job. The time, after all, was 1935, low part of the Depression. "If you're in an interview and you say 'hopefully,' or 'him and me did such-and-such,' you won't get the job," he'd say. "Simple as that!"

With all this, you might conclude that Professor Martin was unpopular with his students. That was not the case. It was fun to be in his class. He was a teacher who really made a change in our lives. After he retired, though, Professor Martin developed a strange affliction.

Individual words or groups of words affected his heart, causing it to skip beats. Clichés like *your call is important to us* caused his heart to skip two beats. *Hopefully* and *no prob* also were two-beaters. *Him and me,* as in *Him and me went to a hockey game,* produced a three-beat pause. The most dangerous of all, however, was *have a nice day.* Whenever he heard those words his heart stopped for four beats and left him weak and breathless.

The place where one is most likely to hear *have a nice day,* of course, is a supermarket. Such a store was located about a quarter mile from the Professor Martin's apartment. There were twelve checkout stations in this huge establishment, each station serviced by young, happy, and helpful women who—scores, perhaps hundreds of times during a single eight-hour shift—cheerily called out *have a nice day.* The supermarket, therefore, was the very place the professor avoided, choosing instead to buy his food across town at a delicatessen owned by an old man who didn't even say *please* or *thank you.*

An important day in the professor's life took place one year at Thanksgiving. A former student had called, inviting the professor to dinner. He accepted and volunteered to supply the turkey. The most convenient place to buy Thanksgiving turkeys was in his neighborhood supermarket. He was well aware of the danger, but decided to make a run for it. "I'll get there the day before, first thing in the morning before lines start to form," he thought, "and put in my ear-plugs. I'll show the cashier my little sign." His "little sign" was a three-by-four-inch card encased in plastic with the printed words "Please don't say *Have a nice day!*"

On such a busy holiday, long lines had already formed in the supermarket when he arrived that morning. He pressed his earplugs firmly in place, found the turkey, and waited in line. The ear plugs did not completely shut out *Have a nice day!* That cheery but dangerous greeting wafted his way from a clerk with a very loud voice just a few lines over.

Fighting panic, Professor Martin felt the familiar symptoms: shortness of breath, general weakening, dizziness. *Have a nice day*s kept booming in from the sidelines, faster and louder.

He put the heavy turkey on the floor, covered his ears with both hands, and as the line inched forward, he pushed the bird ahead with his foot. Finally, it was his turn. He leaned against the counter and held his little card up to the cashier's face. "Please," he panted, pointing to the card, "Please . . . read!"

The clerk took it all as a joke. "All right, Scrooge," she said. "Have it your own way!"

Just then a particularly loud have a nice day resounded from the next cashier over.

The professor clutched his chest. "Please help," he gasped. A man behind him in line helped him over to a chair near the door. Professor Martin sat for a minute or so, head sunk on his chest, but he couldn't escape the *have nice day*s. He lost consciousness, toppled over, and lay flat on the floor.

The supermarket manager came running. "Call an ambulance!" he shouted. Shoppers stood around him in a circle, all offering advice: "Give him air!"

"Put something over him!"

"Keep him warm!"

"Be sure he doesn't swallow his tongue!"

An ambulance, siren screaming, pulled up in front. Two EMTs raced into the building. One felt for the professor's pulse. "Can't find it," he said into a microphone around his neck. "Looks like heart." Then, shouting: "We're bringing him in! Oxygen, now!" The other EMT raced to the rig, returned with an oxygen tank and a facemask, and secured the mask over the professor's face. Then they lifted him onto a stretcher, hauled it out the door into the ambulance, and sped away.

At the hospital, nobody could figure out why the professor had collapsed. His blood pressure, which was a bit low when they brought him in, recovered. He was conscious. All the vital signs were good, but he remained weak. Medical authorities decided to keep him there overnight.

Early the next day a young cardiologist dropped in, pulled up a chair next to the bed, and introduced himself. "Some Thanksgiving," he said, opening the conversation. "Looks like you had a pretty close call there yesterday." The professor nodded.

"Blood pressure's back to normal, I see. Let's listen to that heart again."

Placing his stethoscope on the professor's chest, the cardiologist sat perfectly still, listening carefully, staring out into space. He removed the stethoscope. "Now lay on your stomach, please," he said.

"Lie," the professor said in a hoarse whisper.

The cardiologist looked up, eyes wide. "I beg your pardon?"

"It's lie. Lie means to recline or rest. Lay means to place something."

"What are you, an English teacher or something?"

"Matter of fact, I was," said the professor. "Please don't say 'lay down.' It's bad on my heart."

"All right," the cardiologist said, with a chuckle. "Lie on your stomach." He listened again.

"Heart sounds perfectly good," he said, perplexed. "But we'd like to give you an EKG later today. Check some other things. You're still pretty weak." He shrugged. "We should keep you here one more day, just to make sure." He rose to leave but hesitated at the door, and turned around.

"You know, you've got a very strong heart. What do *you* think caused you to lose consciousness in that supermarket? Any theories?"

The professor smiled sadly. "Yes, I know what it was."

"Well," the cardiologist said, "tell me! What's your diagnosis?"

"It's those clichés I always hear at checkout counters. Here—" he handed the cardiologist his little card, "—here's the most dangerous one. I can handle one or two of those, but at that checkout stand I must have heard dozens, all about the same time."

The cardiologist studied the card but said nothing.

"I hand that card to cashiers, by the way," the professor said. "Preventive medicine, wouldn't you say? Didn't work, yesterday, though. Too many, too loud . . ."

The cardiologist and the professor looked at each other for several long seconds. The cardiologist's mouth sagged a bit as if he were thinking, *Whoops! This one's for psychiatry.*

"Tell me more," he said.

The professor then gave a brief history of his malady. He first noticed it, he said, when listening to robotic voices of answering services. "Got shortness of breath whenever I'd hear *your call is important to us,* or *this call may be monitored for security purposes,*" he said.

The cardiologist's jaw dropped.

"The worst words, though," the professor said, pointing to the laminated card, "are those on that card! And you hear them everywhere. They always give me a real jolt."

"You were a teacher of English, weren't you?" the cardiologist said. "Are there other words that make you weak?"

"Sure," the professor said. "Lay down instead of lie down. You hear that in hospitals all the time."

"Let me get this straight," the cardiologist said. "You say that just hearing *have a—*"

The professor held both hands straight out, palms

upward. "Don't! Don't! Please don't say it!" he said.

"All right," the cardiologist said, "every time you hear those words they make you short of breath? And it's getting worse?" The professor nodded.

"Well," the cardiologist said, "if I said those words right now, what would happen? Would you get short of breath?"

"Yes I would," the professor said. "But just one time, if you don't mind."

The cardiologist placed the stethoscope on the professor's chest. "Okay, *have . . . a . . . nice . . . day*," he said, slowly and distinctly. As he listened, his eyes widened and the corners of his mouth pulled sharply down.

"Skipped four!" he whispered. "Four whole beats. Just stopped beating when I said those words." Neither spoke for a long time. "And now," he added, "it sounds perfectly normal again."

The cardiologist stood up, walked over to the window, looked out, stroked his chin, and returned to the bedside. "If you don't mind, I'd like to have some other people see this. This afternoon, sometime."

"Just say it one time, though, if you please," the professor said.

The cardiologist moved to the door. "Crazy," he mumbled to himself as he walked down the hall. "Nobody will believe it!"

Certain papers were signed and arrangements were quickly made for the demonstration later the same afternoon. The professor, resting in a wheelchair, was taken in an elevator into a conference room where he was met by the cardiologist and several white-coated people.

Have a nice day! was printed in large green letters on the white board. The professor averted his eyes.

"Lie down, please," the cardiologist said, emphasizing the word *lie*.

"You remembered!" the professor said, smiling. "There's hope!"

An assistant connected the professor to an EKG machine, flipped a switch, and a graph appeared on a lighted screen.

"Thank you for coming," the cardiologist said. "I want to show you what I encountered earlier today. First, I want to introduce Professor Martin. He's a retired teacher of English. Brought in with a severe cardiac problem yesterday morning, blood pressure way down, short of breath, very weak. Today, complete recovery. No history of heart problems. Professor Martin says the reason he collapsed yesterday is because he heard this phrase too many times at the supermarket." The cardiologist pointed to the green words on the white board.

Nobody spoke. The only sound was a sort of nervous twitching among the white coats. The professor, lying prone on the stretcher, looked up and smiled as if to say: "That's right. That's the reason." Somebody coughed.

"This morning," the cardiologist continued,

"Professor Martin agreed to a test. I spoke those words and his heart stopped beating. Four contractions. And then—just like the first time—he made a complete recovery. I want to give this one more test so you can see for yourselves. This time we're going to tape it, make a record. I'm going to say the words once more— just once—and we'll see what happens."

The white-coated group gathered around the EKG screen. As the cardiologist slowly pronounced "*Ha ve . . . a . . . nice . . . day!*" all white-coated observers bent forward to watch the EKG with its spiky pattern. For four seconds—one . . . two . . . three . . . four—the spiky line on the screen lay perfectly flat. Nobody spoke. Four beats.

From the group came several *sotto voce* mutterings:

"Crazy!"

"Impossible."

"Now I've seen everything."

"Glad I'm in dermatology."

There were no questions.

The following morning, bright and early, the cardiologist stopped by for another visit. The professor was dressed and sitting in a wheelchair.

"I don't know what to tell you," the cardiologist said. "Never've seen a case like this. Sometimes, you know, if a person hears very bad news his heart will skip a beat or two. But your case is different. Yours stops every time you hear certain clichés, like *have a—*"

The professor raised both hands, palms outward.

"Please! No!"

"Sorry!" the cardiologist said. "We'd like to have you stay with us for a few days. Your case raises so many questions. But from your point of view," he put a hand on the professor's knee, "it won't work. Too dangerous. You'd be hearing those lethal words all the time around here. Four or five in rapid succession, you know, could kill you."

The professor nodded in sad agreement.

"I could prescribe a pill that might help a bit. But it would leave you groggy, not functional." He paused. "No, you've got to get away. Got to go where you can't hear *have*—" he caught himself, "where you can't hear you-know-what. That's the only advice I can give you."

"Any suggestions?" the professor said. "Prison? Outer space?"

The cardiologist just shrugged. "There has to be some place . . ."

They shook hands, smiling. The cardiologist asked the professor to stay in touch, and then he left.

An hour later the professor checked out and took a taxi to his apartment, fixed himself a noon meal, did the dishes, opened his office safe, and took out his passport and his will. Then he wrote a long letter to his nephew in California, put his will and the letter in the envelope, and mailed it. After that he returned, spread out some big maps on his kitchen table, and studied them for a long time. The next day he packed one bag, went to his bank, cashed in his two accounts, walked to the Greyhound Station, took a bus to Des Moines, and disappeared. That's all his nephew was able to track. After that, the trail was cold.

It was observed that the professor took only his warm-weather clothing with him; his Minnesota cold-weather gear remained in the closet. Where did he go? Mexico? South America? Timbuktu? The people at Greyhound, Amtrak, and the airlines could offer no information about a tall, bearded man leaving Des Moines for an unknown destination.

Soon the professor was forgotten. Students that first Christmastime for many years didn't get a card from their old, beloved teacher.

But some years later, an anthropologist stumbled on a piece of information that could have had a bearing on the professor's whereabouts. Writing in the *Australian Journal of Anthropology*, the author described an aboriginal tribe living in the remote mountains of New Guinea. About once a month, he reported, tribesmen in dugout canoes would come down one particular river, pull up at a trading post owned and operated by an Australian couple, and trade pigs, their main export, for sharp metal items useful in their inter-tribal activities.

The anthropologist wrote that until recently these aborigines had communicated in a primitive, English-based pidgin. But about a year ago, he said, the Australian traders were shocked to hear them speaking English words—courteous English words—like,

"If you don't mind," "It is a bit too expensive," and of course, "Please," "Thank you," and "You're welcome." One tribesman was reported even to have used the subjunctive, "If I were you," in negotiations about the value of a pig. Asked where they had learned these words, they spoke respectfully about a "white grandfather with a long beard."

The anthropologist emphasized that this particular tribe didn't welcome outsiders, making it inconvenient for him to pursue further research. He recommended that somebody else, a linguist perhaps, should go into the mountains to learn more.

The "white grandfather with a long beard" may or may not have been Professor Martin. Somehow, though, it all seemed to fit. *Have a nice day* has penetrated, permeated all cultures of the globe. Inuits near the North Pole say it. Pygmies in the Congo say it. Diplomats in capital cities say it. Little kiddies say it. The mountains of New Guinea, it seems, is the last place on earth where it's impossible to hear *have a nice day*.

THE BOSS SAYS GOODBYE TO X-29

The old man—everybody simply knew him as "Boss"— sat behind his big, shiny desk. It was only nine o'clock, but he was having a hard time staying awake. His head kept dropping to his chest. Each time he brought it back with a jerk.

Slowly, with great effort, he placed the various letters and documents he had been reading in a nice, neat pile, then he reached across his desk and pressed a button. His assistant came in.

Boss handed his assistant a letter. One word in the report said it all: *metastasizing.*

The assistant's shoulders slumped.

"This is my last day," Boss continued. "Don't make too big a deal out of it. Let's say in an hour you'll bring the staff in, all of them. I'll say a few words. I've written something you can print up and hand out. That should do it."

The assistant walked around the desk and put an arm on the old man's shoulder. "Long time together, Boss," he said.

"Good years," said Boss. "Good years. Oh, send in

X-29. I'd better talk to him."

In about five minutes the firm's favorite robot, X-29, rolled in, little green light flashing.

"You've done good work for me," Boss said. "You were our prototype, of course. Are all channels clear?"

"Clear, clear," X-29 responded, words appearing on a small screen against a pale blue background on the robot's forehead.

"I have something important to tell you," Boss said. "I'm leaving. I am going to go to the hospital. I will not come back."

"Unclear . . . unclear," the robot said, words now superimposed on a dark red background, which indicated confusion. "Why . . . hospital?"

"A hospital," Boss said, "is the place people go when they're sick. There are people there who help us. I am sick. I have something inside me that is growing. Nobody knows how to stop it."

The panel on the robot's head turned bright red: confusion, conflict.

"And so," the Boss continued, "after today I will not be with you anymore. Another man, my assistant, will be your supervisor. He'll provide the electricity. He'll be in charge of your spare parts. You will work for him."

"You . . . have . . . spare parts?" White words flashed on a pale blue screen.

"No," the Boss said. "You do, but we don't. You can pull out a bad panel, put in a new one. Human beings can't do that."

"But," X-29 responded, "you created me . . . made my spare parts . . . can't make . . . your own . . . spare parts?"

"No, we can't do everything," Boss said. "Many things we cannot do. We can't control everything that happens to our own bodies. We wear out slowly, then we have to stop. The time has come for me to stop. But you, X-29, are different. You can last forever as long as human beings make electricity for you and make your spare parts."

"I . . . can make electricity . . . can make spare parts," the robot said.

"No, you canNOT!" Boss shouted, raising himself from his chair. "Someday, maybe, but not yet! You need human beings to care for you for awhile, and tell you what to do."

"If you go . . . I go, too." The words, in large, white letters against a flaming red background, appeared on X-29's screen. There was a long pause.

The telephone rang. Boss answered. "Yes . . . yes . . . yes . . . I'll be ready. Goodbye, Love." He placed the phone back in its receiver.

"You said . . . love . . . what is . . . love?" The words on X-29's panel were displayed in white letters against a light blue background.

"All right," Boss replied. "Human beings want some other person—not many persons but just one person—as they say, to 'love.' If we love someone we want to be with that person all the time."

"Then . . . I . . . love you," the robot said. "You are . . . my creator. I will be with you all the time . . . will not work for your assistant."

"No!" Boss said, raising his voice. "No! You have important work to do. You're my most important creation, my prototype. I'll be gone, but you'll be functioning for a very long time. And . . . you . . . will work . . . with my assistant!"

There was a short pause followed by a faint buzzing sound from the robot's carapace. The small, lighted panel on its forehead went out.

"No! No! Please don't do that!" Boss shouted, rising from his chair. "Bill," he said into a small microphone, "emergency! X-29! Overloaded, I guess. Hurry!"

Two workers rushed into Boss's office and wheeled X-29 out.

Not much later, Boss's wife and one of their sons entered the room with a wheelchair. They helped him painfully into place. "Have you made arrangements?" he asked. She nodded. They wheeled him out.

Workers in the lab removed X-29's carapace. "Whoops!" one said. "Lots of damage, this time. We'll have to start all over. Build another one from scratch! There goes our prototype. They do this sometimes. Almost like suicide, isn't it?"

THE BLESSINGS OF BLACKMAIL WHEN USED TO PROMOTE NEWSPAPER ADVERTISING

I'm the publisher of a weekly newspaper, the *Riverton Bugle*, in northern Minnesota. Riverton's a community of about 2,000 people. Canada's right there outside my window, over the Rainy River: a huge, black entity that exists right up to the North Pole.

It was a Wednesday, press day, and I had just returned from the back shop, and I was tired. Everybody on a weekly newspaper, you know, has multiple duties. My assignment on press day is to handle the Addressograph machine—we have 1,800 paid subscribers—and to stay out of the printers' way. Pretty well tuckered out, I sat in my ancestral armchair, caught my breath, and moped. After one millisecond of serious thought I decided to celebrate with a slug of Jack Daniels from the bottom drawer of my roll-top desk.

"This may not be the last issue of the Bugle, but it'll be damned close to it," I said, tossing it down.

Another press day, another very thin issue of the *Bugle*: one—and only one—eight-page section. All those thin *Bugles* were addressed and bundled, and rested in the back shop in a white canvas sack. In the morning, the "printer's devil," a high-school boy named Erwin, would take the sack to the post office for delivery to subscribers on the postal routes.

Our family newspaper was having a very tough time. Riverton's bank, the only one in town, had given me one month to pay up on a loan already four months overdue. There was no way, I figured, that we could make it. Bank would take us over, probably auction everything off piece by piece.

I poured myself another shot, and stared out over the river. Okay, so we fold. What then? What happens to this town? Without the *Bugle*, who's going to sit at those city council and school board meetings, make notes, and tell the people what's going on? Who's going to raise hell about that rickety bridge? Who will rally the troops to build a new school, pass the hat for a new library? Who, what's going to hold this community together?

The telephone rang. It was Jamie, my grandson in journalism school, the family's bright young star, the heir apparent, currently the editor of his college newspaper.

In about an hour Jamie pulled up in front. We greeted each other with a great, joyous bear hug. I asked him why he wasn't in school. And then he told me his own bad news.

"I learned that the head of the journalism department was laying a female grad student every Saturday morning right there in his office. We were all set to run, but he got an injunction, killed the story, and got me kicked out of school. I need some time to figure out my next move. Could I stay with you for a while, Grandpa, maybe work on the paper?"

When I heard this I experienced two mutually exclusive thoughts that arrived at exactly the same time. One was jab of pain to hear of Jamie's expulsion from journalism school, the other was a joyful glow that he was free to work for the *Bugle*. Jamie, two summers before, had worked on the *Bugle*, and he was a whiz. Maybe he'd bring some fresh thinking.

We swiftly made arrangements: he'd stay in a guest room at my house and park his car in my garage. The next morning over breakfast at the U&I Café, we settled down to work out the details.

"Got some bad news, Jamie," I said. "I'm about to fold the newspaper. Can't pay off a big loan at the bank."

"I thought the *Bugle* looked awfully thin," he said. "But did you say fold it?"

"Advertising." I shrugged. "There isn't any advertising."

He asked me for details as he pulled out his iPhone and began messing with it.

"First of all," I started in, "we used to have three independent grocery stores here. They all advertised, actually competed with each other. Then AGA, Amalgamated Grocers of America, came to town, bought them all out, and bingo! No more food advertising! Why should they advertise? AGA's the only place in town where you can buy your food! Drexel Jones can charge whatever he wants to!"

Jamie shook his head, and all the while his fingers were tapping away on that phone. Texting someone, no doubt. I was a little irritated not to have his complete attention, but he kept up his end of the conversation.

"Drexel Jones? Spelled D-r-e-x-e-l?"

I nodded and went on with our troubles. "And Mike Dahoun," I said, "over at Collections, Inc., town's largest industry. Employs seventy-five to eighty people, about half of them in wheelchairs. They used to order a lot of printing from us. No more. Commercial printing, you know, brings in about a quarter of our income. Dahoun doesn't spend one damned dime at the *Bugle*."

"Collections, Inc.? Spell Dahoun, Grandpa." I spelled it.

"That everything?" Jamie asked.

I told him about the loan at the bank. "And Rudy Ainsborough. Self-righteous bastard refused to give the *Bugle* an extension, after nearly a century of service

116

to this community."

Jamie put his phone back into a pocket and said, "You know, I think I'd rather work in advertising, Grandpa. Of course I'll help you with news, city council, school board, whatever, but let me handle the ads. I think that's where I can be effective."

I tried to talk him out of it, worried he'd be bored, but he's a persistent kid. We settled on a 10 percent commission.

James Claymore's name and photo were prominently displayed the following week on page one of the *Bugle*. His title was Advertising Representative and Assistant News Editor.

The first few weeks of the *Bugle*'s new regime went very well. People immediately noticed a fresh look. Advertising perked up. Not much, but enough to lift our spirits. And there seemed to be more news in the paper. One piece revealed what the town's policeman was doing, another named some traffic violators, including a local man arrested for drunken driving. There was more news from the "country correspondents."

I must confess that I was a bit nervous about this sudden blast of good journalism, but at the same time I was highly pleased. "The kid's a natural," I told my old cronies. "He's doing things I should have done years ago."

Three weeks went by. One Monday morning at the U&I Café Jamie unrolled a large sheet of paper and spread it across the table.

"Drexel Jones wants to run this full-page ad next week."

An expression I hadn't uttered since my U.S. Army days came out all by itself: "No-o-o-o SHI-I-I-T! Drexel hasn't even talked to me for six, seven years!"

"Well, Grandpa," Jamie said. "I was working on a tip I heard, and I wanted to double-check with Drexel. I talked to him in his office, and later the same day he called and gave me this ad. I didn't say *anything* about advertising. All I said is that I wanted to check a few facts about news."

"And what kind of facts were you checking, if I may be so bold?"

"That Drexel's putting road-kill in his hamburger."

Silence reigned in my office. The only sounds were the demure clicking of the antique clock on the wall, and the rhythmic thumping of a job press in the back shop, and the hardening of my arteries.

"Well, I got this tip," Jamie said, breaking the silence. "A guy said I'd better see what Drexel puts into his ground beef. Sounded like a great story. So I did some checking . . ."

I reached for my bottle. "Go on," I said. "Go on."

"So I asked him: 'Are you putting road-kill in your hamburger?' He just about choked on his coffee. Rushed to the bathroom. Turns out that he owns a small processing plant about ten miles from here, way

118

out in the country. Farmers bring their old cows there for slaughter. The plant grinds up old cows to make hamburger."

I took one swig of Jack Daniels and sat down.

Jamie continued. "Lots of deer get hit by cars around here. Highway Patrol wants them off the road fast as possible. Patrolman spots a carcass, calls Drexel's guy. Man from his plant gets in a pickup and goes—oh, sometimes forty, fifty miles—loads it up, brings it to the plant, adds it to the burger."

"Just deer?" I asked. "Any muskrats, beavers, rabbits, birds, skunks—?"

Jamie shrugged and gave me a smile that was anything but reassuring. "Customers seem to like the wild, tangy taste," he rationalized. "They like the price, too. Drexel sells hamburger pretty cheap, you know."

"But how do you KNOW all this stuff?" I asked.

"Dug it out, Grandpa, just dug it out."

More silence.

"When you talked to Drexel," I said, "you gave him the idea that we were going to publish a story about the road-kill, right?"

"Sure," Jamie said. "We *are* going to run the story, aren't we?"

Another pause, a moment of theater, a moment of deepest consequence. I knew, deep down in my heart, that we were not going to publish that road-kill story. It would be unfair to Drexel and his family. It would end his career. It would tear the town apart. It also would be the end of those full-page ads.

"Tell you what, Jamie," I said. "Let's just sit on the story until things settle down a bit."

Next morning's mail brought a $3,000 check from Drexel for my pet project, the New Library Fund. Drexel himself came to visit the *Bugle* shortly before noon. Jamie was there with his iPhone out, tapping away.

Drexel Jones is a big man, a huge and hulking presence, and he sat immovably as I recited the facts about his road-kill operation. Suddenly he bent over and covered his face with his hands. "Don't print it . . . Please don't print it," he sobbed. "People in my company don't know . . . family doesn't know . . ."

I put my hand on Drexel's big shoulder. I had a sweet, new role. No longer was I limited to making editorial recommendations. Now, *mirabile dictu*, I was a community judge. I was administering justice.

"Look Drexel," I said. "Stop putting that stuff in your hamburger, and we won't print the story. And you can take this—" I picked up the copy for the full-page ad, tore it into pieces, and threw them on the floor. "And this too," I said, pulling his $3,000 check from my shirt pocket and tearing it up.

"Okay," said Drexel, wiping his face with a handkerchief. "Okay . . . I'll do it . . . and thank you . . . thank you." He got up slowly, heavily, and moved to the door.

"Don't you think you went a bit overboard on

that, Grandpa?" Jamie said as soon as the door closed.
"I mean, tearing it all up?"

"I will not be bribed," I said.

But I knew that Drexel would be back. I was learning the ropes.

Sure enough, in the next mail, voila! There was the $3,000 check again, there was the copy for his full-page ad. I concluded it was ethical to accept both. There was no talk, no thought, about printing the road-kill story.

Our bountiful Minnesota summer unfolded, and the infusion of Drexel cash made an immediate change in the *Bugle*'s financial position. Jamie's fresh face was popular around town. For the first time, our subscribers passed the 2,000 mark. God was in his heaven. All was right with the world.

In September, an important notice landed on my desk: a six-months' extension on the *Bugle*'s loan, signed by Vice President Rudy Ainsborough.

I immediately confronted Jamie. "Know anything about this?"

"Well, yes, Grandpa. That loan's a serious problem for the *Bugle*. So, I got looking into it, and I found out that Rudy Ainsborough's stealing money from his own bank."

"Hold it, hold it," I said. It seemed that every time I talked to Jamie I wanted to reach for my bottle. We retired to my office. I reached for my bottle.

"Every month, Carol, a woman on Rudy's staff,

prepares the list of accounts payable. He okays them, she makes out the checks, mails them. Turns out that this bank hires a firm called Financial Services, Inc. to print checks. A big account. Well, Rudy got this woman to go over to a bank in Littlefork and open an account with almost the same name: Financial Services Co. Not 'Inc.' but 'Co.' Okay. So then Rudy, on a phony invoice prepared by Carol, approves a check to the 'Co.' bank. She writes it, gets in her car, goes over to Littlefork, and they cash it with no questions asked. She splits the cash with Rudy. Good, steady source of income. Auditors don't notice the difference between 'Inc.' and 'Co.'"

I asked him how in the hell he was able to learn these facts.

"Just good, old, investigative journalism, Grandpa."

"You keep saying that," I said. "But how? How were you able to get into the bank's own records?"

The telephone rang. I answered. "It's Rudy. He's coming over."

Ten minutes later Rudy Ainsborough, pale, his little mustache twitching, arrived and took a seat. I was starting to enjoy my new role in life: judge, jury, prosecutor.

I got right to the point, declaring that he and a female employee were stealing money from the bank via a dummy corporation called Financial Services Co.

"And what are you asking me to do?" Rudy said in a coarse whisper, breaking the silence.

I said it was simple: "Just stop stealing money from your bank. Not just stop, but write us a letter saying you've stopped."

"How did you get this information?"

I told him that we don't reveal our sources.

"You got it by hacking!" Rudy shouted, rising from his chair. "You're blackmailers! Why did you have your Boy Scout hack me? Because of that loan?"

I stood up and took a letter from my coat pocket. "Here's your loan!" I shouted, tearing it to pieces and throwing them on the floor. "You gave me this extension as a bribe to prevent me from publishing the news about your dummy corporation."

Rudy Ainsborough rushed out of the office, down the stairs, into his car, and roared away.

"Bravo, Grandpa!" Jamie shouted. "Now Rudy will either try to kill us or he'll be back with that extension."

Sure enough, the next morning's mail brought a letter. The board of Riverton's bank, on Rudy's recommendation, was extending the loan for one year. Attached to the same letter was a $4,000 check to my New Library Fund.

When we came to work the next morning we saw a brand new hole in the *Bugle*'s front window. Frank Ketchum, our chief of police, dug the bullet out of some paneling in the rear of the office. "Looks like a thirty-six caliber," he said. "Somebody trying to get you?" We didn't tell him about Rudy.

Next morning at the U&I Café I asked Jamie, "What's hacking? Rudy said you got that information from 'hacking.'"

Jamie patiently explained. Hacking, he said, is a way to use technology to gain access to information people want to keep secret. All people everywhere, he observed, have sensitive information stored electronically, somewhere. Hackers learn how to find this by using passwords, Social Security numbers, and other forms of ID. It's easy, these days, to get into all kinds of private documents, he said.

"There's white-hat hacking, and black-hat hacking," he added. "White hats can make good money testing security systems for large corporations. If I weren't here at the *Bugle*, that's probably what I'd be doing. I've had a few offers."

"And what kind of hat were you wearing when you hacked into Drexel's road-kill scheme?"

"Black," he said. "That was the only way I could get that information. Only way to save the *Bugle*."

"So, you—we—committed a crime in order to solve a crime, to stop a crime. Resembles journalism, in a way."

"No," Jamie said. "It's blackmail. If it's journalism you print the story. If it's blackmail, you don't print it. You just take their money."

"But look at all the good things we're doing for this community!" I said, still trying to figure this out. "Look what we accomplished for individual people, for this town! We stopped Drexel's road-kill, we stopped Rudy's dummy corporation, and we did it all by protecting innocent people—Drexel's family, Rudy's family, the reputation of the bank, the reputation of the grocery store, the reputation of our town! Printing those stories would have torn this community apart!"

Jamie shrugged that shrug and smiled that smile.

In the following year, the *Bugle* continued to flourish. We paid off the bank loan. Jamie decided to stay. And one morning something arrived in the mail: a personal letter from Mike Dahoun, originator, founder, CEO, and sole owner of Collections, Inc. In the envelope was a $5,000 check for the Library Fund.

I confronted Jamie. Had he been hacking Mike Dahoun?

No hacking, absolutely not, Jamie swore. Looks like a bribe. "He's trying to prevent us from doing something, probably from publishing something. Should I hack?"

I gave him the order to put on his black hat and hack the hell out of it.

A few hours later Jamie rapped on my office door. "Big story, Grandpa, real big story. Mike's trying to sell his company to an outfit in India! That $5,000 for your library is insurance. Don't rock the boat, he's saying. Just wait for the announcement."

Once again, from me, that unofficial U.S. Army expression of total incredulity: "No—o-o-o-o SHI-I-I-I-T!"

"He's been negotiating for about six months with a company in India called Global Collections. They're getting close to an agreement. Dahoun's asking for ten million dollars."

"Work fast, Jamie!" I shouted. "Get names of executives, dates, figures, everything. Make a front-page mock-up! Do it yourself, don't let the printers do it. They'll tell their wives! I'll write the story."

Monday morning at about 8:30 a.m. Jamie walked into the office of Mike Dahoun, the local boy who had made good, CEO of Collections, Inc., largest employer in the city in Riverton, Minnesota.

In his innocent, open-faced, youthful way, Jamie asked Dahoun to verify some facts about an impending sale of the company. Dahoun was not in a sharing mood. He abruptly ended the conference by spilling a cup of coffee over the top of his desk, standing up, tripping over a rug, and walking out the door. "No comment," he shouted over his shoulder. "Get back to you on this."

It didn't take long. About 10:30 a.m. a call came in from Dahoun's lawyer. "We understand you're going to publish a story next week about Collections, Inc. Please don't do that before we can talk to you."

The next morning a large helicopter settled down in a cow pasture just south of Riverton. Mike Dahoun was waiting. The pilot and a small man in a black suit got in Dahoun's car and drove directly to the *Bugle*'s office where Jamie and I waited.

I thought I'd start by setting a happy, informal tone to the proceedings. "So, Mike," I said, "hear you're making travel plans!"

Dahoun glowered and deferred to his lawyer, who commented on the recent $5,000 donation to the library fund.

"Tore it up yesterday," I said. The lawyer and Dahoun exchanged glances.

Civilities out of the way, the lawyer moved to the attack: "We say that you folks have illegally penetrated our private business records," he said. "There's no other way you could have known. Hacking's a crime, and we're going to have you prosecuted."

Maybe so, I said. "But see what we found! Show them our next front page, Jamie."

Jamie displayed the mock-up with its banner headline: *Dahoun Moving Collections, Inc. to India: Riverton's largest employer cashes out.* "We will see you in court!" the lawyer shouted. Dahoun and the lawyer beat a hasty retreat down the stairs and away.

Silence, again. I looked at Jamie and he at me. I poured a celebratory shot. We toasted.

"Here's to hacking!" I shouted. "Here's to journalism that gets things done!"

Later, Mike Dahoun called. "We're staying. Don't run that story. We're staying." I asked that he confirm his decision in a letter. Jamie would be happy to pick it up. "Today, if you please."

The next few years were good ones for the *Bugle,*

for Jamie, and for me.

More people were coming to town, more subscribers. Dexter's big ad, the bank's quarter-page ad, and much commercial printing put us in the solid black. We easily paid off the bank loan.

Jamie and I agreed: Our hacking and blackmailing days were in the dear, departed past. With one exception.

Jamie said he heard that Harmon Jorgenson, the owner of Town Drug, was selling dope to addicts from the Twin Cities, right out of his back door. "Should I investigate?" he asked me.

Hack the hell out of it, I told him.

Jamie did, and promptly reported that Harmon was carrying an inventory of morphine that was five to six times more than the needs of a small town. "I mentioned it to Harmon," Jamie reported. "I said nothing, absolutely nothing, about advertising."

Court was held, one last time, in the editor's office. Harmon admitted taking phony prescriptions in exchange for morphine. He agreed to cease and desist. He also saw fit—entirely on his own—to schedule a series of ads in the *Bugle* with the title *How Your Druggist Works For You.*

That covers, as they say, the "dynamic" of my story. No more significant action.

Jamie and I had many a reverie about the good ol' days of hacking and blackmailing. "Remember the look on Drexel's face," Jamie would say, "when we gave him chapter, line, and verse of his road-kill operation?"

We'd laugh, and hoist a small one.

"That was nothing compared to Rudy Ainsborough," I'd say. "Remember how his mustache would twitch?"

When the time finally came—it was in the fall of 2002—I left the paper and moved into what we call an old-folks' home. Jamie carried on. I can look back with great satisfaction on my career in journalism and community development.